'Are you spoiling for a fight, Dr Mason?'

His blue eyes flashed with challenge.

Kim raised her eyebrows at the tone of his voice. 'Are *you*?'

Once more, he seemed determined to stare her down, and Kim wasn't about to back away. She glared into those blue hypnotic eyes and felt a wave of excitement buzz through her body. He looked down at her lips and Kim felt her breathing increase before his gaze returned to meet hers. Her own eyes widened in total disbelief at what she saw there. *Desire?* Surely not. They hardly knew each other.

POLICE SURGEONS

**Love, life and medicine—
on the beat!**

Working side by side—
and sometimes hand in hand—dedicated
medical professionals join forces with
the police service for the very best
in emotional excitement!

From domestic disturbance
to emergency-room drama, working to
prove innocence or guilt, and finding
passion and emotion along the way.

UNDERCOVER DOCTOR

BY
LUCY CLARK

MILLS & BOON®

To my Year 11 teacher, Jim, who always told me to believe in myself.
Ps 56:3

First published in Great Britain 2004
Large Print edition 2005
Harlequin Mills & Boon Limited,
Eton House, 18-24 Paradise Road,
Richmond, Surrey TW9 1SR

ISBN 0 263 18468 4

Set in Times Roman 15¾ on 17 pt.
17-0705-53203

Printed and bound in Great Britain
by Antony Rowe Ltd, Chippenham, Wiltshire

CHAPTER ONE

'CLAMP,' Dr Harry Buchanan ordered as Kimberlie Mason continued to watch the operation in awe. She knew all about Dr Buchanan, MB, BS, Ph.D, Fellow of the Royal Australasian College of Surgeons. He was one of Australia's leading general surgeons and now here she was, in the same theatre as him, watching him operate on the Foreign Minister from the small Pacific island country of Tarparnii.

'Swab,' he ordered, and Kim was once more delighted at the deep, rich resonance of his voice. She glanced up from her position on the opposite side of the operating table to look at him. Every part of his face was protected from infection but the clear shield that covered his eyes didn't hide the dark blue pigment that surrounded his pupils.

Kim saw a movement in her peripheral vision and turned her head slightly. John McPhee, the anaesthetist, was changing over the saline bag. It had been a long and involved operation, one which she could tell by a quick glance around the room most personnel were beginning to feel.

'Suction, Dr Mason,' Jerry Mayberry, Harry's registrar, instructed. Kim brought her attention back to the task at hand and did as she was told. It had been a long time since she'd been in an operating theatre as spick and span as this one, though not so long since she'd operated. Nothing of the calibre of Harry Buchanan, but Kim had medical experience these people would never know about.

'Right. Everything looks fine here. Give me a check X-ray.' Harry stood back from the table, his hands held up. Jerry and Kim followed suit and once more Kim's gaze was drawn to the man who was the Master of Ceremonies in this operating room.

Her heart flipped in surprise, finding Harry's gaze on her. She tried hard to read his expression while at the same time trying to quash the emotions he was able to stir with one simple look. During the five days she'd been working at Sydney General Hospital, this was about the closest she'd been to the man who commanded respect from all his staff.

Rising to the challenge she saw in his eyes, she didn't break the contact but forced herself to concentrate harder. *Keep your objectivity.* The words echoed around in her mind. It was what she'd been trained to do.

The radiographer had everything in position when an ear-piercing alarm echoed around the room.

'John?' Harry glanced at the anaesthetist, waiting for the answer.

'V-tach,' John called.

The theatre was a hive of activity as every member of the team rallied together to save the patient. The sickening feeling in the pit of Kim's stomach intensified. It was just as she'd been warned. The Foreign Minister of the Tarparnii government was at risk of assassination while he was in Australia. Did that include having a heart attack on the operating table? A *planned* heart attack?

She ripped the drapes off the patient as one of the theatre nurses handed Harry the defibrillator paddles.

'Clear!' Harry called, and everyone stood back as he placed the paddles on the patient's chest and sent an electric surge through the supine body.

'Still in V-tach,' John called, after checking the monitor.

They increased the voltage.

'Clear!' Harry commanded, and again sent a pulse through the man's body.

'No change,' John replied.

'Again,' Harry called, and waited for the change in voltage to be made. 'Clear!'

Kim held her breath, praying the Minister's heart would start beating again.

'Asystole.' John's tone was almost as flat as the line now showing on the screen.

'Again,' Harry instructed.

'Harry,' John said. 'It's no good. He's gone. Call it.'

'Clear!' Harry sent one final pulse coursing through the patient.

'He's gone, Harry.' John's tone was final and firm. 'Call it,' the anaesthetist urged.

Harry handed the paddles back to the theatre nurse and glared at John. 'Time of death—sixteen twenty-five. *What happened?*'

'I'm checking.' John took notes from the dials in front of him. 'Everything was fine—and then the flat-line.'

'Myocardial infarction?' Harry queried in disbelief. Kim was watching the two men intently. The atmosphere in theatre was one of incredulity at what had just transpired and uncertainty at the chief surgeon's reaction.

'People have been known to suffer heart attacks on the operating table before, Harry,' John responded.

'Not on *my* operating table.' Every word was said with complete clarity. 'And *not* a foreign diplomat.'

'First time for everything,' Jerry Mayberry said softly into the silence that ensued. Unfortunately for the registrar, Harry heard and spun around to face him. Kim held her breath, wondering what would happen next.

'Leave everything exactly the way it is,' Harry directed, his piercing blue gaze sweeping the people before him. 'Don't move, touch or remove *anything* from this theatre. You should all know the hospital's protocol for a death in surgery. Follow it to the letter. Get changed and report to my office immediately.' With that, Harry stripped off his gloves and theatre garb before waiting for everyone to follow suit.

He stood by the door, glaring at each and every member who walked past him out of the room. Kim was the last one and as she passed by he said, 'One moment, Dr Mason.'

Kim stopped and looked at him.

'Tell me again how you managed to be in my theatre this afternoon?'

'I swapped this operation with Dr Edington as his wife's car broke down and he had to pick up his children from school.'

'So you volunteered to help him out. Very… convenient for you.'

'Actually, *he* came to *me* and asked me to swap.'

'Yet you jumped at the chance.'

'Yes.' Kim raised her chin, a hint of defiance in her eyes. 'Despite what I think about you personally, you *are* a brilliant surgeon. As I've only been at this hospital for a week, I took the opportunity to see the great Harry Buchanan in theatre.'

'Your résumé said you haven't had much experience.'

'I'm a service registrar. The bottom of the ladder. Most service registrars when they first start a surgical rotation haven't had much experience in Theatre.'

'Then I must say you coped rather well today.'

'I pay attention. Now, if you'll excuse me?'

Kim took a few steps away from him but stopped again when he continued. 'I find it…coincidental that the first time you're in my operating theatre, my patient dies.'

Kim turned to face him. 'What's that supposed to mean?'

'I've worked with every other member of that team before.'

'So because I'm new and there's a death, you're going to blame me for it? The man had a heart attack.' Kim spread her arms wide, palms facing upwards.

'You believe that, do you, Dr Mason?'

'I was there. *You* were there.' Kim narrowed her gaze. 'What are you trying to imply? That he *didn't* die of a heart attack?'

'I've never lost a patient on the operating table before,' Harry retorted, his words strong.

'Well, you just did. Stop trying to blame someone for it, Harry—especially me.' Ignoring his raised eyebrow at her familiarity, she turned and walked away, heading for the female changing rooms. She shook her head and grimaced, unable to believe she'd actually called him by his first name. How unprofessional!

She went into the changing rooms, then stopped just inside and opened the door a little, watching the corridor. Where was Harry? She'd half expected him to be right behind her yet it was a good forty-five seconds later when he appeared in the corridor. She shut the door. Why had he stayed behind? Was he trying to conceal or remove evidence? Was the great Harry Buchanan involved in what had just happened with the minister?

Kim pondered these thoughts as she started to change. Because of her talk with Harry, the other female members of the theatre staff were almost all ready so she dressed with greater speed than usual.

'You'd better hurry up, Kimberlie,' the theatre sister said. 'If there's one thing Harry Buchanan dislikes, it's tardiness.'

'That and a few other hundred things,' Kim mumbled.

The other woman chuckled. 'You've been here, what, one week? I think you have a fair idea of how the boss works. He doesn't forgive or forget.'

'Yeah. Look at Elaine—after what happened with her, I doubt he'll ever date another woman from the hospital again,' another nurse chimed in.

'Who's Elaine?'

'Oh, you'll meet her in a minute. But poor Harry, he doesn't seem to have much luck with women,' the theatre sister whispered. 'Rumour has it he was married about ten years ago but his wife was a bigamist!'

'Really?' Kim made sure she acted surprised. Of course, she knew the details about his marriage as they had been in his dossier. She had dossiers on several people at the hospital who were connected with the island nation of Tarparnii and it was her job to covertly investigate each one.

'Ooh. I can't believe you haven't heard this story yet. She was a policewoman, a detective or something like that, and she'd go on these stake-outs and undercover assignments for weeks at a time. All the time, she was cheating on him.'

'That's disgusting,' Kim retorted, smoothing her white top down and buttoning her khaki shorts.

'Since then,' the sister added as she walked towards the door, 'Harry goes ballistic if anyone lies to him. It's better and easier to tell him you've made a mistake or done something wrong than cover it over with deception.'

'Can't say I blame him.' Kim slipped her feet into her flat shoes and headed out the door with the other women, pulling the pins out of her hair and fluffing her fingers through her shoulder-length red curls. She glanced at the other women who were all chatting away as they walked towards Harry's office and quickly slid a subvocal earpiece/transmitter into her ear.

'Anyway, I can't believe that Minister Japarlin actually died on the operating table,' she said to her colleagues.

'What?' came a voice through her earpiece.

'I don't think Harry's going to get over this. He's never lost a patient on the table before,' one of the nurses muttered. 'He's going to be even more impossible to work with.'

'He has a temper?' Kim asked.

'Uh, not really. He just clams up and he's all business and sometimes that makes for a strained atmosphere.' They opened the door to the stairwell and started up the stairs.

'Kim,' came the male voice through her earpiece. 'I can't get through to Ivan in the morgue. Give him a call to let him know he's on.'

'Oh, hey, don't say that,' Kim said to the women. 'You're making me nervous about working with him.' She grimaced. 'I think I need to go to the bathroom.'

'He's not that bad,' the theatre sister said, and eyed her cautiously. 'You're not going to throw up, are you?'

'Oh, no. No. Nothing like that. Just a weak bladder, that's all.'

'Don't take too long. The debriefing's going to start very soon. I don't want you getting into trouble with Harry so soon after starting.'

Kim smiled and went back down the stairs. 'Thanks. I'll be quick.' She headed in the direction of the toilets they'd passed a few seconds ago where she'd seen an internal phone on the wall.

She picked it up and dialed the extension for the morgue. 'Hi. This is Dr Mason,' she said when the call was connected. 'Can I speak to Ivan, please?'

A moment later, Ivan came to the phone.

'He's dead,' was all she said.

'Copy that.' Ivan disconnected the call.

'All done,' Kim said for the benefit of her earpiece, and headed back to the stairwell.

'Thanks, Kim. Must be something down there that interferes with Ivan's earpiece.'

There were footsteps behind her and Kim glanced over her shoulder. She veiled her surprise at seeing Harry there but she didn't say a word. At the top of the stairs, she felt his arm brush hers as he reached past to hold the door. Tingles flooded through her body at the minor touch and she baulked at the involuntary attraction.

'Thank you,' she mumbled. As she breathed in, the scent of his aftershave teased her senses. He smelled good. He was dressed in his usual uniform, a dark suit, crisp white shirt and college tie. He looked good, too. Kim licked her lips as she continued down the drab corridor, acutely aware of his close proximity behind her. Neither of them spoke.

Kim could feel the way his gaze swept over her figure and her breathing became shallow. She exhaled slowly in an effort to control her emotions, which had temporarily gone haywire. When they finally entered his office, it was crowded with people—some who had been in Theatre and others who hadn't.

Harry quickly scanned the room before nodding to a tall blonde woman who was wearing an impeccable black suit. She made Kim feel quite dowdy.

'I think we'll get down to it. There are some new faces here so I'll introduce myself.' She glanced at Kim as she said the words. 'I'm Elaine Parkinson and I'm the hospital's investigation co-ordinator. Any death in this hospital is thoroughly researched, wherever it might have taken place.'

Ah, so *this* was Elaine. Kim looked at the other woman. She didn't seem to be Harry's type. Not that she herself was the expert on what type of woman Harry Buchanan liked—far from it. She hardly knew the man. She gave herself a mental shake and focused on what Elaine was saying.

'As you are all aware, the patient in question was Mr Japarlin, the Minister for Foreign Affairs for the Tarparnii government. The authorities have been informed and the forensic science team has already been called to Theatre. The sooner we can have the theatre sorted out and cleaned, the sooner we can get it back into operation again, pardon the pun.' She laughed mockingly at her own little joke.

'You will all be required to give statements so, apart from that, as the death appears to be due to natural causes with no suspicious circumstances, the investigation should be completed within the next seventy-two hours.' Elaine's smile was false as she looked around the room at the staff gathered there.

Kim glanced at Harry. His expression hadn't changed. He was still scowling, obviously peeved that his patient had dared to die on his operating table. Come to think of it, ever since she'd started working at this hospital, in his department, she hadn't seen him do anything other than scowl. A smile tugged at Kim's lips as she wondered whether she should tell him that if he stayed that way too long, his face would stick.

She realised then that he was scowling at her. The smile and the thoughts which had prompted it vanished as Kim brought her attention back to the drivel still coming out of Elaine's mouth.

Red tape, red tape, red tape. If there was one thing Kim didn't like about her job, it was the mounds of red tape which always had to be waded through. Everything by the book, as Moss, her real boss, always said. Though Harry Buchanan was her boss as far as the hospital was concerned, Kim had been sent to Sydney General Hospital to investigate medical personnel who were linked with Tarparnii. The Australian Secret Intelligence Service had received information that an attempt was going to be made on the minister's life, as Tarparnii was currently in the midst of political and civil unrest. Her previous assignment had been operating out of an army tent in a war zone, so being in a nice, properly sterilised theatre was quite a step up in the world of medical espionage.

When the police arrived, Kim gave them her statement, mindful of her ASIS cover. There was no need to tell the police what she was really doing at the hospital. Her investigation for ASIS was on a federal level, but these police were state-based. She knew the forensic science team would do their usual thorough job but she also knew Ivan would do an even better one.

Thanks to Elaine Parkinson's little speech, it was clear the hospital intended to treat the Foreign Minister's death as having been from 'natural causes'. Yet Kim wasn't convinced. Neither, it seemed, was Harry Buchanan, if their earlier conversation was anything to go by.

Once the police had finished with her, Kim went to the hospital cafeteria and sipped thankfully at a strong cup of black coffee. The cafeteria was bustling with people as they rushed to eat some dinner before either going home or back to work.

Taking the cup with her, she crossed to the house phone on the wall, dialled the morgue again, asking for Ivan.

'Debrief's all done. Official position is natural causes. What's next?' she asked quietly.

'Come back around eight. I'll let you in.'

'Okey-dokey.' Kim took another sip of coffee as she replaced the receiver. She turned and walked straight into solid muscle, her coffee spilling everywhere.

She gasped. 'I'm so sorr—' The words choked in her throat as she looked up into Harry Buchanan's blue eyes. She knew she could drown in those eyes and quickly forced herself to look away.

Kim looked down at the crisp white shirt he was holding away from his skin so the hot liquid didn't scald his flesh. A hush settled over the cafeteria and most people were looking at them before whispering to one another.

'Dr Buchanan,' Kim began again, unable to believe that out of all the people in this room, she'd had to dump coffee on *him*. 'I'm so sorry. It was an accident.' She held her breath, trying to gauge his reaction.

'Hmm.' His tone was filled with repressed mirth as his gaze swept lightly over her body. 'At least I'm not the only one covered in coffee.'

Surprised to discover he had a sense of humour, it took a second for his words to sink in. Kim followed his gaze down to just below her breasts where there were a few dark droplets staining her white top. She felt a deep heat begin to rise from within her at the feel of his gaze upon her body. Trying to control the increase in her heart's rhythm, Kim licked her suddenly dry lips. The cup and pool of liquid at their feet was forgotten.

She looked up at him again. 'So it would seem.'

'You two OK?' a nasal voice asked beside them, and both turned to look at an elderly woman dressed in the uniform of the cafeteria staff, holding a mop. 'Don't ya worry about it, lovies. I'll clean it all up for ya. Go and rinse yaselves down, now. Go on. Off ya go before it stains.'

'Thank you,' Harry and Kim mumbled at the same time. Kim looked at him, a frown piercing her brow. Surely he couldn't be drop-dead gorgeous, a brilliant surgeon *and* have manners and a sense of humour? She shook her head and smiled. She must be mistaken.

'Something funny?' he queried as they walked out of the cafeteria.

Kim shook her head. 'No. Look, Dr Buchanan, I really am sorry.' She needed to find her professionalism again.

'Back to formalities?'

Kim glanced up at him and was amazed to see the scowl gone. He was even more handsome without it! 'Formalities?'

'After Theatre today, you called me Harry.'

'Did I?' Kim feigned innocence. After all, she was here as a junior member of staff and even though the hospital had a general air of informality about titles she still should address Harry by his until they knew each other better. The problem was, she'd read the dossier on this man, along with those of other SGH staff, a few weeks ago and ever since then she'd been…intrigued by him. She *thought* of him as Harry. No wonder she'd said it. 'I apologise.'

'Leave it.' He shrugged as they turned the corner, heading towards the department.

'Then why did you bring it up?' she mumbled, and could have bitten her tongue.

Harry stopped in his tracks and Kim followed suit. 'Are you spoiling for a fight, Dr Mason?' His eyes flashed with challenge.

Kim raised her eyebrows at the tone of his voice. 'Are *you*?'

Once more he seemed determined to stare her down and Kim wasn't about to back away. She glared into those hypnotic eyes and felt a wave of excitement buzz through her body. He looked down at her lips and Kim felt her breathing increase before his gaze returned to meet hers. Her own eyes widened in total disbelief at what she saw there. *Desire?* Surely not. They hardly knew each other.

There was barely any distance between them and Kim became aware of their very public surroundings. Clearing her throat, she stepped back.

'I have to go. I apologise again for the coffee.' It was a real struggle for Kim to meet his gaze but she did so before walking off down the corridor. She entered the stairwell and took the stairs down to the hospital's basement. In a dark corner she pressed her fingers to the pulse at her wrist and practised deep breathing while she waited for it to return to normal. Nothing—in all her training—had prepared her for the likes of Harry Buchanan and the unwanted effect he had on her equilibrium.

She sighed and looked at her watch, forcing all thoughts of Harry from her mind. She had work to do and there was no place in her life for any sort of distractions, especially not in the form of her new boss. She was an intelligence operative and she had a mission to complete.

'Kim?' the voice in her earpiece said. 'Everything OK?'

'Yes. Are we having the theatre bins collected? Once the forensic guys are finished and the scrub nurses have cleaned the theatre, we should grab those bins.'

'I'll get it organised,' came the reply.

Kim looked down at her coffee-stained clothes. 'I'm going home to change and then I'll meet Ivan.'

'OK. I'll go back to head office and give Moss an official report.'

'Mason out,' she said and removed the earpiece. Checking her watch once more, she headed out the hospital, switching on her mobile phone as she walked the short block to the train station. Thankfully, the trains ran every few minutes and she didn't have to wait too long for hers to arrive. It was just after seven o'clock and the warm summer evening sky boasted the pinks and reds of another beautiful sunset.

'"Red sky at night, shepherd's delight,"' she quoted to herself as she punched the elevator button in the lobby of the serviced apartment block where the agency was housing her for the duration of her assignment.

Kim walked in and stripped off her stained clothes before getting beneath the spray of the shower. She tried to focus on what she needed to do but her thoughts kept returning to Harry Buchanan and the look of desire she'd witnessed in those amazing blue eyes.

Turning the water off, Kim was rubbing her hair dry when she realised her phone was ringing. She flicked open the mobile and answered it.

'Dr Mason.'

'How's it going, Kimmy?' her best friend, Tammy Jones, asked.

'Not bad.' Kim's thoughts briefly flicked to Harry. 'How was your day?'

'Good. I just wanted you to know, I've been assigned to you.'

'Great. How did you manage to swing that?'

'It wasn't hard. Besides, after I saw the dossier on Harry Buchanan, I knew you'd be in trouble and need a friend there to help watch your back.'

'What do you mean?'

'Oh, come off it, Kim. The man's gorgeous. How could you not fall into his arms if he opened them? No. You need someone who knows you really well to help with this mission.'

Kim laughed, wondering if Tammy could read her thoughts. 'He is pretty good-looking but not my type.'

'What *is* your type?' Tammy said the words softly. 'Come on, Kim. You've refused to date anyone I've offered to set you up with for the past two years.'

'We have completely different taste in men, Tam. I'm not into your heavy rockers covered in piercings and tattoos.'

'You've got to look beyond all that,' Tammy said. 'Anyway, my point is that this Harry looks as though he could cheer you up.'

'Or if he's the one who murdered Japarlin, I could get a lot more than I bargained for.'

'Hey—take a chance!'

Kim shook her head. 'I did that once before and got my heart broken.'

'Chris died four years ago, Kim. Four years! And it wasn't your fault. You know that, don't you?'

'Yes, Tammy. We've been over this ground so many times. Anyway, I'm supposed to be meeting Ivan at eight in the morgue so I'd better go.'

'Ooh. Now, that's what I call a hot date.' Tammy giggled.

'Yeah, right. I think Ivan's wife might mind. Did you get the message about the theatre bins?'

'All organised and I'm expecting them soon.'

'See? This is what makes a good team. Communication. I don't know why Moss doesn't keep us as a permanent team. You and I work well together, Tam.'

'I think Moss is starting to realise that. Do you need me to be monitoring you when you're in the morgue?'

'No. Should be fine. I'm just having a look and, besides, Ivan's there.'

'Call me when you're done. Oh, I also wanted to let you know your mum called the ghost number twice today.'

'I know. She's left three messages on the mobile. I've just stepped out of the shower and was going to call her but…' Kim glanced at the clock again '…I have to rush out. I want to get a look at the body and I'm also on call tonight.'

'She's worried about you Kim,' Tamara said seriously.

'Not physically. She wants me to settle down and have a family. I'm only thirty-two but, according to her, you'd think my ovaries have completely shrivelled up and are incapable of producing any more eggs.'

'She wants grandchildren. It's no fault of yours, it's just what parents want as their children get older. You're their only child, Kim. They want you to settle down.'

Kim heard the repressed laughter in her friend's tone. 'This is funny? You think this is funny?'

'Hey, you were the one who wanted to work with me.' Tamara laughed out loud. 'Hang up now and give her a quick call. Put her mind at rest.'

'OK. Gee, Tammy, you nag almost as bad as she does.' Kim finished dressing while she spoke. 'Look Tam, I have to go. Thanks for ringing.' Kim ended the call and quickly applied her make-up. She was dressed in black trousers and a black sleeveless knit top. Collecting her hospital identification and pager, she grabbed her phone and keys and shoved them into her backpack before heading out the door.

When she stepped outside, the stars were beginning to show themselves. Kim took a taxi back to the hospital, calling her parents briefly on the way. Yes, she was fine. No, she wasn't dating anyone. No, she wasn't free for dinner this weekend but, yes, she was free the following weekend. Would she be bringing someone with her? Probably not but she promised her mother she'd let her know if things changed.

Kim smiled and shook her head as she ended the call. She knew she was loved and it was a nice feeling, but she couldn't live her life according to her parents' wishes. If they knew she'd been working with ASIS for the past five years, they'd probably suffer dual heart attacks. All they knew was that she was in the army—which helped explain all the travelling she did—and that alone caused them enough worry. She didn't want to add to it.

She hated deceiving her parents but in the circumstances it was an act of love to lie to those who meant the most to her.

Kim walked into the hospital, greeting people as she went. Service registrars worked all sorts of hours so no one thought it strange she was there. She walked through the hospital and out to the back where the morgue was located. The security guard was on duty but Kim wasn't worried. She continued walking out the door that led to a small grassy area next to the hospital chapel. Rounding the corner, Kim headed for the rear door, the one where deliveries and pick-ups of cadavers were made out of sight of the general public.

She checked her watch and tapped lightly, four times, on the door. Within seconds it opened. She nodded to Ivan before he closed the door behind them. Kim rubbed her bare arms as she followed him through to where the minister's body was stored.

He pulled out the drawer and pointed to a torch on the bench.

'Have you had a good look yet?' she asked Ivan.

'No time. I'll do it later when it's quieter.'

'OK. Give me five minutes.'

Ivan nodded and left her alone. Kim pulled on a pair of gloves and reached for the torch. She wasn't quite sure what she was looking for, but some sort of clue as to what had really happened would be great.

She tried hard to think back to what had happened in Theatre and for the life of her she couldn't remember anything that had been out of the ordinary. She was engrossed in what she was doing but also conscious of the fact that Ivan would be back soon, so when she heard a shoe scuff on the floor behind her, she simply whispered, 'Your watch must be fast.'

'Really?' drawled the deep, rich voice she was beginning to know so well. Prickles of apprehension rippled down Kim's spine as she straightened. 'So tell me, Dr Mason...'

Kim swallowed nervously and turned—slowly—to look directly into the handsome face of Harry Buchanan.

'What's a nice girl like you doing in a place like this?'

CHAPTER TWO

A DOZEN thoughts went through Kim's mind in the split second she stood there, staring at Harry. He'd changed his clothes, but she hadn't expected anything else after she'd dumped coffee all over him. He was now dressed more casually than in the suits he'd worn all week.

The dark blue polo shirt made the colour of his eyes more intense and the denim jeans which clung perfectly to his shape almost made Kim hyperventilate. She forced her gaze back up to meet his. What *was* she doing here? That had been his question. She decided flippancy might be her best cover.

'Well, you know…' She shrugged nonchalantly, as though his presence hadn't disturbed her in the slightest, and pivoted back to the cadaver. 'It's difficult for a girl my age to meet nice men nowadays.'

He didn't laugh. 'How old *are* you?'

'Thirty-two.'

'Really? You look about eighteen.'

'I'm going to take that as a compliment. How old are you?'

'Thirty-eight. Now that we have that out of the way, would you mind telling me what you're doing here?'

'What does it look like?' Kim shone the torch up the arm which still contained the IV line. When a patient died on the operating table, all tubes were cut off rather than removed from the patient's body. After the forensic pathologist had ascertained the cause of death, everything would be removed.

Kim moved to the other side of the drawer. 'How about you? What brings you here at night?'

Harry walked closer to the drawer and peered down to where she was shining the light. 'I don't think he died of a heart attack.'

'I agree.'

'You do? You didn't earlier today.' They were both quiet for a moment while Kim directed the beam of light into the wound Harry had been about to close moments before the patient had died.

'Everything checks out,' Kim mumbled, and looked across at him. 'What you said after Theatre got me thinking. I wanted to come down here and take another look.'

'So you just waltzed in here and helped yourself?'

'Apparently. Did you want to look at anything specific?'

Harry shook his head in confusion. 'I keep going over that moment in my mind. Had I accidentally severed an artery? Was something left inside the patient?'

'Neither. Take a closer look.' She held the torch out to him. Harry pulled on a pair of gloves and took the torch. Kim moved away.

'What's wrong?' Harry didn't look up.

'Hmm?'

'You're nervous, uneasy.'

'Maybe it's you. Maybe you make me uneasy.'

Harry looked up then and smiled at her. 'I doubt that. You don't appear to be afraid of me.'

'Should I be?'

'I guess not, but most other service registrars are.'

'And I'm different?' She took off her gloves and disposed of them.

'You have...a confidence not usually found in someone just starting out in the surgical field.'

'I'm also older than the average service registrar,' she pointed out.

'Yes. Why is that?'

She shrugged, searching her mind for a blanket statement which would get her out of this pickle.

'Not everyone goes to medical school straight from high school.'

'So…' He took off his gloves and tossed them in the bin. 'If you're not uneasy about me, that means you're uneasy about our friend the Foreign Minister here and the events surrounding his death.'

Kim sighed. 'I don't know what it is that's making me nervous. It's just a feeling. Intuition, I guess.'

'Things just don't add up.' Harry nodded and cut the light. He pushed the drawer back in. 'This really isn't the place to discuss it. Come back to my office.' Harry headed for the door and Kim went after him. In the corridor, she saw her contact mopping the floor. She nodded to him as she walked past—right out the front door of the morgue, in front of the security guard who said nothing but a brief goodnight before focusing on the small television behind the desk.

They were both silent as they walked through the empty corridors which led to the general surgery department and Harry's office. Once there, he flicked on the light and indicated a seat. Kim sat down, watching the assured way he walked around his desk before sitting opposite her.

'Why don't you think he died of a heart attack?' she asked, before he could say a word.

'Because he was a fit and healthy man.'

'He was in his sixties—surely his age put him in a high-risk category.'

'His age had nothing to do with it. He didn't smoke, he rarely drank alcohol. Had no family history of heart disease. He ate sensibly and exercised regularly.'

'Fair enough.'

'How about you? What's your reasoning?'

'It seems a little…convenient that he would die of natural causes on an operating table when he was—as you've just pointed out—in good physical shape.' Kim stood up and started pacing the room. 'I mean, the man has been accused of crimes against his people.'

'There's been no evidence,' Harry pointed out.

'No, there never is. Most politicians are able to hide things,' she said, her tone impartial and logical. 'Anyone who tries to dig up the dirt is…taken care of. Before he had the Foreign Minister portfolio, he was in charge of the military and that episode out at Barhana where all those natives were *accidentally* killed—well, that type of situation lives long in people's minds. Ethnic cleansing, I believe the politically correct term is. Needless to say, Mr Japarlin had a lot of enemies.'

'You sound like a Tarparniian sympathiser.'

'Aren't you?' Kim stopped pacing. She looked at him intently for a moment before raising one eyebrow questioningly. 'You go to Tarparnii—what, once or twice a year? Why couldn't Mr Japarlin have had his surgery done then?'

Harry's gaze narrowed. 'You certainly know a lot about my activities.'

'Well, it's hardly a secret, Harry.' Kim spread her arms wide. 'Everyone in the hospital knows you go over there.'

'And although you've only been working here for one week, you've found out a lot of information about me.'

'You're not the only one I've heard gossip about, but you are close to being one of the main topics.'

'Gee, thanks,' he remarked dryly.

'Oh, I'm not trying to flatter you, I'm just stating facts. Look, Harry, people talk. That's it. I just happened to be in the room when they were talking and sometimes it's a bit hard not to listen. Do you want me to tell you *everything* I've heard about you? Will any of it come as a surprise?'

'Drop the subject.'

'Why? You're the one who brought it up.'

'You're becoming annoying, Dr Mason.'

Kim smiled, not taking offence at his words. 'Thank you. It's one of my best qualities.'

'I'm sure your parents must be very proud,' he drawled, desperately trying not to be impressed by her. She wasn't like his usual service registrars and she also wasn't like the other women he worked with. She was…fun. She didn't mince words and she didn't back down from an argument. He admired that. It showed she wasn't afraid of the truth. He also realised he liked the verbal sparring they'd been doing, glad she had a sharp brain beneath the mound of red curls on her head.

Her hair was tied back, as it had been every time he'd seen her during the week—except when she'd been in Theatre today. Then she'd had it pinned in a bun. Since he'd first laid eyes on his new service registrar, Harry had felt a tightening in his gut. Kimberlie Mason was a beautiful woman. It was a statement of fact. He'd kept a close eye on her during the week, telling himself it was strictly professional as she'd transferred to his department from a hospital in Canberra in mid-rotation. That in itself was unheard of. Nevertheless, it had happened and as far as hospital administration were concerned, Kimberlie was his new service registrar.

'Harry?'

He quickly looked away, conscious he'd been staring at her. He shuffled some papers around on his desk and cleared his throat, knowing full well her green eyes would be twinkling with merriment when he looked at her again.

'Back to your initial question—why didn't I operate on Mr Japarlin in Tarparnii? It's because he knew he'd be in Australia for the Commonwealth Heads of Government Meeting, which is to be held in three weeks' time. He *chose* to have the surgery done here. My overseas clinics provide a higher level of surgical care to people who otherwise wouldn't be able to afford medical treatment.'

'Very noble of you, Harry.'

He met her gaze and found it intense. He ignored the way it made him feel. 'I'm not looking for justification, *Kimberlie*. I believe that treatment should be available to everyone regardless of social status or income. *That's* the reason why I hold clinics. I also go to Papua New Guinea and Thailand, not just Tarparnii.'

'When were you last there?'

'What is this? An inquisition?'

'Merely a question,' Kim replied, and thought she'd better watch herself. The last thing she needed was Harry uncovering her cover!

'*I* should be the one asking *you* questions.' He rose from his chair and walked slowly around the desk. 'What were you doing in the morgue? How did you get past Security?' His gaze narrowed as he leant against his desk and folded his arms across his chest. 'How did you manage to get into my theatre for the operating list?'

'You *are* full of questions.' There was no way Kim was going to confess to anything, least of all how the agency had tampered with her colleague's wife's car so that Dr Edington would ask Kim to take over his operating session while he collected his children from school.

'Did you kill him?'

Kim looked at him with incredulity before she realised he was serious. Deadly serious. She had wanted to ask Harry the same question.

When she didn't answer, he continued. 'Is that why you were in the morgue? To cover up some vital piece of evidence?'

'I could ask the same of you,' she retorted. 'But for the record, no, I didn't kill him. I would, however, like to find out who did.'

'That makes two of us.' Again their gazes held and Kim shifted from one foot to the other.

'Did *you* kill him?'

'How could I possibly have done that? Everyone was watching everything I did. I was the leading surgeon. If I'd done something wrong, everyone would have known about it.'

'Answer the question, Harry. Yes or no.'

He paused and made sure he looked directly at her when he answered. 'No.'

Kim let out the breath she'd been unconsciously holding. 'I'm pleased to hear that.' He was still a suspect on her list but what he'd said made sense. If he'd made one wrong move, everyone in that theatre would have seen it. Unless he was working with an accomplice. She filed that thought away.

'Another event,' he continued, 'which increased my suspicions that something wasn't right was the disappearance of the theatre bins from Mr Japarlin's operation.'

'What?' Kim frowned. 'How do you know?'

'The instruments made it to the central sterilisation department but the waste bins never arrived at the waste disposal department.'

'That *is* odd,' Kim agreed. She should get an Academy Award for her performance. 'I wonder what happened to them.' She looked closely at Harry. 'What do *you* think happened to them?'

Again he stared at her for a moment and Kim hoped her gaze didn't give anything away. Finally he shrugged. 'I have no idea, but it does prove that Mr Japarlin's death was no freak of nature.'

'He might have picked up a staph. infection while he was here.'

'He was admitted this morning,' Harry pointed out. 'I did a complete health check on him before John McPhee saw him for his pre-anaesthetic review. The man was in excellent health.'

'Still,' Kim reasoned, 'regardless of how hard hospitals try for infection control, "freaks of nature", as you termed it, have a way of happening.'

'You had a look at him in the morgue and so did I.' Harry raised his voice slightly in frustration. 'There was nothing out of the ordinary.'

'No apparent *visual* discrepancies,' Kim pointed out logically, surprised Harry was getting a bit hot under the collar. 'Why does it mean so much to you?'

Harry raked a hand through his hair and exhaled harshly. 'There's just something…wrong. Very wrong. It *wasn't* a freak of nature and it *wasn't* a heart attack.'

'That leaves murder, Harry.' Her voice was soft and she watched as he nodded slowly. Both of them were silent for a whole two minutes, absorbing the enormity of the situation.

Kim sat down and stared into space, unable to believe this man had been willing to investigate things on his own. He had no idea what he was getting himself into and now she felt responsible for ensuring he stayed out of danger. She sighed, knowing it would mean explaining the situation to Tammy and probably Moss as well. Harry was still a suspect so she'd have to keep her wits about her.

'Are you all right, Kimberlie?' His tone was quiet and gentle and she looked up to find him gazing at her, concern in his eyes. 'It's pretty shocking, I know, but sometimes these things happen.'

Kim bit her lip to stop the involuntary smile from spreading across her mouth. Oh, he was so cute when he was being sensitive. It was clear he'd misinterpreted her thoughts, possibly thinking she was afraid of the conclusions they'd drawn.

She opened her mouth to speak when her pager beeped against her waist. A second later, Harry's beeped as well. They both checked the number.

'Accident and Emergency?' she asked, and he nodded. 'Me, too. Looks as though we're in for more fun.'

Harry quickly packed his briefcase and locked his office before they headed down to Emergency and spoke to the A and E registrar in charge.

'Multiple MVA. Two patients already in. Dr Mayberry and Dr Edington are taking one to Theatre, the other has gone off to Radiology.'

The wail of an ambulance siren coming closer could be heard. 'And here's our next delivery.'

'Let's take a look.' Harry pulled on a white gown to protect his clothes and reached for a pair of gloves. Kim did the same and was right behind him.

'Eighteen-year-old male,' the paramedic said as the patient was wheeled into A and E through the emergency doors. 'Driver of second car at MVA site sustained blunt trauma. Hasn't regained consciousness, no pain meds given. Oxygen one hundred percent, IV saline administered. Abdominal abrasions, ecchymosis, lacerations and possible fractured pelvis. Patient has voided with bloody urine, no vomit as yet.'

As the paramedic spoke, the young man was wheeled through to Trauma Room 1 and the nurses began cutting his clothes off and covering him with warmth blankets.

'Haemaccel, stat, nasogastric tube to decompress the stomach and prevent aspiration of vomitus. Get a CT scan organised immediately,' Harry ordered. Once the patient's clothes had been dealt with and Harry had clear access to the abdomen, he had Kim assist him in applying pressure bandages to control the bleeding. 'Vitals?' Harry asked.

'BP and pulse pressure decreased, breathing rapid, pupils equal and reacting to light.'

While they waited for the patient to return from Radiology, Harry went over what he expected to find. 'From the report from the MVA site, this kid was cut from the wreck after being squashed in like a sardine, trapped with the steering-wheel pressing into his abdomen.'

'The pelvis didn't feel too stable,' Kim added.

Harry shrugged. 'Unfortunately, it's all too common with MVAs. Why can't these kids slow down on the roads? They get their licences and think they're invincible.' He thumped his fist against the wall. 'Bladder is obviously ruptured, probably small intestines, but goodness knows what else.'

They'd changed into theatre scrubs and were just waiting for a page to say the patient was on his way back from Radiology, so they knew when to start scrubbing. Harry's pager beeped a minute later and after a word with the anaesthetist and a quick look at the scans, they headed to the scrub sink.

'Let's see how fast you learn, Doctor.'

'With you as my teacher, I'm looking forward to it, *Doctor*.' She flashed him a smile, squashing the feeling of guilt that she was deceiving not only the hospital but Harry about her qualifications. ASIS had felt it better for her to pose as a service registrar rather than a consultant—despite her higher qualifications. That way, she'd be less alienated from other hospital staff lower on the ladder and could therefore take a more objective view of things while she investigated.

Now, though, when there were people's lives at stake, she wondered whether that hadn't been an oversight. Instead of assisting Harry with a procedure, she was more than capable of doing the procedure herself. Still, the hospital was adequately staffed but if the worst came to the worst, Kim knew she wouldn't risk another human being's life just for the sake of her cover. She was a doctor, first and foremost.

'I'll try and explain things as best I can, but if there's anything you don't understand, I'd prefer you to ask.'

'Yes, Doctor.'

'It will be interesting to see how well you cope.'

'Yes, Doctor.'

'At your old hospital, how many hours a week did you spend in Theatre?'

'The average for a service registrar, Doctor. Far too many.'

Harry glanced at the nursing staff around them before looking at Kim. She winked at him quickly before concentrating on what she was doing. He choked as he swallowed, then coughed, unable to believe his new service registrar had just winked at him. Did that constitute flirting? He wasn't sure. Had he enjoyed it? Yes, he had!

He returned his thoughts to the job at hand, determined to push the woman beside him to the back of his mind.

The operation began with removing the pressure bandage and Harry discussing what he was going to do. 'According to the CT scan, there is a rupture to the urinary bladder, the small intestines and, if we look up a little, a laceration to the liver.'

The surgery went well. Harry continued to explain things and Kim asked a question here and there to make it look authentic for him. She watched him with wonder. He had finesse. His gloved hands were steady in their work and he had the ability to pinpoint problem areas easily and promptly. His style was smooth, direct and neat. No wonder he'd earned the label of being one of the best general surgeons in Australasia.

His pager sounded twice while they were in Theatre. Once, to let them know two other patients had arrived from the accident. One was DOA and the other was being taken to Theatre by Dr Edington, who would like Harry's expertise once he'd finished. The second time his pager beeped was to pass on a message that his patient's name was Tony Donnelly.

'Well, Tony,' Harry said to his patient, after the last drain had been inserted and he was ready to close, 'don't speed, obey the road rules, realise you are mortal—like the rest of us—and, above all, keep out of my theatre because I honestly don't want to see you back here again.'

When they were finished with Tony, Harry degowned and headed into Theatre to help Dr Edington. 'Check out the situation, Kimberlie, and if you're not needed, join us.'

Kim checked with the A and E registrar but was told the situation was now under control. She spoke with the orthopaedic registrar about Tony. 'He's in Recovery and so are his CT scans. Pelvis is fractured in two places—acetabular cup and the iliac crest.'

'Thanks. I'll go take a look at him.' Kim went with him, checking on Tony so she could give Harry an update, before heading to Theatre where she knew Harry was expecting her. She scrubbed and gowned, confident he'd be putting her to work.

'And here she is,' Harry said when she entered the theatre. 'Patient has, among other things, a ruptured spleen which is beyond saving so Dr

Edington here is doing a splenectomy. Have you ever done one before?'

'Would you like me to assist with this one?' Kim asked, deliberately not answering his question.

'How did you guess?' Harry stepped back from the table to allow her access. She could feel him watching her the whole time and although it unnerved her, she worked especially hard to push the thought from her mind so she could concentrate on what she was doing. She gave him the updated report on Tony and told him the situation in A and E was stable as far the general surgical team was concerned.

'Good. I'll contact the orthopaedic registrar about—'

'It's done,' she stated.

There was a pause before he said, 'Good!'

Kim tried not to be pleased at the impressed tone in his voice. She might not be able to see him but she was almost positive his eyebrows had been raised in surprise at her initiative. She took a breath, forcing the thoughts away once more so she could concentrate on her job.

Dr Edington operated in a slow, laid-back manner which was completely different from Harry's. She much preferred Harry's style...and she wasn't just thinking about his operating skills either. She smiled beneath her mask, glad of its cover.

'You did a fabulous job,' Harry said once they were done. He called through to A and E, was told everything was still fine. Together they checked on Tony, and Harry added another scribble to the notes after reading the report from the orthopaedic registrar.

'Time to get changed.' They walked back to the change rooms and went their separate ways. She was exhausted but happy as she changed back into her black clothes. Tammy would be anxious for a report from her and she still had that to deal with when she arrived home.

Refusing to let that bother her, she slung her backpack over her shoulder and headed out of the change rooms, walking slap bang into Harry, his briefcase clattering to the floor. He quickly retrieved it.

'This is becoming a habit, Dr Mason. At least you're not holding a cup of coffee.'

Kim smiled at him as she smothered a yawn. 'Thank goodness Theatre is over and the emergencies have been dealt with.'

Harry nodded. 'Let's get out of here before another round comes in.'

Kim looked at him in surprise. 'I didn't think the boss was allowed to talk like that. What kind of impression is that supposed to give to us lowly registrars?'

Harry placed his hand gently beneath her elbow and started to usher her out. Kim shrugged away, not only because she was mindful of who might see them but also because the touch of Harry's skin against her own was enough to send her system into overdrive. She was so aware of him, it wasn't funny.

'It's OK, Harry. I'm not that tired. I think I might actually be capable of walking.'

He nodded. 'I'll walk you to your car.'

'No, it's OK. You don't need to bother. I'll be fine.'

'I'll walk you to your car,' he said more forcefully, and Kim realised that, despite what she'd previously thought, chivalry was not dead.

'I don't have a car,' she replied softly. 'I'll take a taxi home. There's usually one or two outside the front of the hospital.'

'At this time of the morning? I don't think so, Kimberlie.' They walked out into the cool morning air.

'Ah.' She breathed a sigh of relief and stretched her arms out wide, flinging her head back. 'Cool breeze at last.'

'You don't like summer?'

'No, it's great, but I also like being able to cool off, and after that stint in Theatre, I need to cool off.'

Harry watched her closely. She had the most amazing neck, one which was begging him to nuzzle and kiss it. Clenching his hands into fists, he resisted the urge…but only just. She pulled her hair from the band restricting it and shook her curls free. They floated softly down her back and as she brought her head back up, they settled around her shoulders, framing her face, the rays of the streetlight above bringing out the vibrant green in her eyes.

There was no doubt about it. Kimberlie Mason was a beautiful woman.

She raised her gaze to meet his and, unable to look away, Harry cleared his throat. 'Are you sure you're thirty-two?' His voice was soft, intimate and Kim felt a warmth tingle through her.

A slow smile spread across her lips, one he itched to kiss.

'Yes.'

'You look so young, so vulnerable, so… helpless.'

His words made Kim laugh. If only he knew the truth. He looked hurt and she quickly reached out a reassuring hand to him. 'I'm not laughing *at* you, Harry. That's sweet, but I'm none of those things. Well…maybe a little vulnerable from time to time but generally I have it under control.'

He looked down to where her hand was resting on his arm and she quickly removed it.

'Sorry.'

'No. Don't apologise.' When she'd shrugged away from his touch outside the change rooms, Harry had thought she didn't feel the same tug towards him as he felt towards her, but now she'd voluntarily reached out to touch him. Perhaps his touch on her arm had made her far too aware of him, just as her touch had now done to him.

He broke his gaze from hers, knowing it was the right thing to do, and scanned the road in front of the hospital. 'No taxis,' he said. 'In fact, no vehicles of any kind around at the moment.'

'Give it a few minutes and either an idiot will come speeding past or an ambulance will arrive.'

'As I said earlier, let's get out of here before either one happens. This way.'

Harry started walking towards the hospital car park across the road. Kim merely frowned but didn't move. He turned to glare at her. 'Well, come along, Dr Mason. We can't have you standing outside the hospital in the wee small hours of the morning.' He came back and placed his hand more firmly beneath her elbow. 'The car is this way.'

'You're going to take me home?'

'I am.'

'But I live in the opposite direction.'

'How could you possibly know that?'

Kim clenched her jaw as they continued to walk. How could she have made a slip like that? It was his fault. The touch of his hand on her arm was shooting sparks of longing through her, making it difficult to concentrate. They reached his car and he took a set of keys from his trouser pocket and unlocked the door.

'Thank you. Uh…I just meant that as a registrar, I probably live in cheaper accommodation than you. Not many up-market homes where I live. They're all in the opposite direction.'

Harry headed around to the driver's side and Kim was thankful he was no longer touching her. Perhaps now she could get her brain back into gear.

'That's a highly presumptuous statement to make, Kimberlie.' He opened the rear door and placed his briefcase on the back seat.

'Am I wrong?' she asked, knowing full well where he lived.

'Er…no.' They both climbed in and buckled their seat belts. 'Still, it's no trouble and you'll get home faster if I drop you off rather than waiting goodness knows how long for a taxi.'

'Well, thank you, Harry.' She gave him directions to her apartment and as he drove they talked about hospital life and the surgery they'd just finished. Nice and neutral. When he finally brought the car to a stop outside her well-lit building, he shifted in his seat to face her.

'Kimberlie, about Mr Japarlin's death.'

'Yes?'

'We're going to keep what we discussed strictly between ourselves,' he stated.

'I'll keep it confidential.' She nodded. She'd share the information with Tammy but it would still be confidential.

'Good, because we have no idea what we might be getting ourselves into. The last thing either of us needs is to be caught up in some political problems with the Tarparnii government.'

'Agreed.'

'And as intriguing as it is, if things get too dangerous, Kimberlie, I want your word you'll leave it alone. That you'll just walk away and forget everything.'

'Harry.' Kim gave a nervous laugh. 'You're starting to worry me now.' He was so adorable when he went into protective mode.

'Promise me, Kim.' His words were urgent.

'So long as you promise to do the same.'

He nodded and so did she.

They were silent, staring into each other's eyes. The scent she now deemed synonymous with Harry teased at her senses once more. Kim's breath caught in her throat but she forced herself to relax and breathe properly. She bit her lower lip before her tongue darted out to wet her lips. His hand was gripping the steering-wheel so tightly, his knuckles were going white. She needed to move *now*! 'Well…uh…thanks for the ride.'

He nodded as she opened the door and picked up her backpack.

'I guess I'll see you later.'

'Yes.'

She climbed out and turned to smile at him. 'Be safe now.'

He smiled back, the intense mood broken. 'I will. Goodnight, Kimberlie.'

She shut the door and straightened, waving as he drove slowly away. He watched her in his rear-view mirror until she turned and went inside the building. He stopped at the T-junction at the end of her street and closed his eyes for a brief second.

The woman was irresistible and he was having an incredibly hard time keeping his hands off her. When she'd bit her lip, he'd felt himself begin to capitulate. When she'd wet her lips, it had been almost impossible to suppress the groan of desire he'd felt build within him.

He opened his eyes and turned onto the main road, heading towards the Sydney Harbour Bridge. She was his registrar, a colleague. He'd dated colleagues in the past and it had never turned out well. Did he really want to go down that track again? Was he such a glutton for punishment that he was going to risk putting his heart out there again? He couldn't afford not to, he realised. What if she was the one?

'Kimberlie Mason.' Saying her name out loud only made him want to groan again, and this time he let it flow. In his theatre the previous afternoon and while they'd operated that evening, he'd been extremely conscious of her exact whereabouts at all times. Because of that, he'd noticed how she'd pre-empted most of the requests he'd made while they'd operated and one thing he knew for sure: she was very good. As this was her first year of surgical experience, he knew she'd have no trouble with the rest of her training and would make an excellent general surgeon. So why had her résumé said she had little experience?

Harry prided himself on giving credit where it was due and Kimberlie had certainly impressed him tonight. It made him wonder what she'd done before pursuing medicine. Had she been a nurse? That might explain her aptitude for things. Had her medical career been interrupted somehow, perhaps with the death of a loved one? As she was approximately five years older than the average service registrar, perhaps her life experiences had made it easier for her to adjust and adapt.

'Too many questions,' he mumbled as he drove the car into the car park beneath the North Shore building. He retrieved his briefcase from the back seat and headed over to the lifts.

She appeared to be fitting into the department without complications. Jerry Mayberry, his senior registrar, was Kimberlie's immediate superior and the two seemed to have hit it off well. In fact, on Wednesday afternoon, at the busy departmental meeting which was attended by all and sundry who had anything to do with the general surgery department, he'd noticed Jerry saving a seat for Kimberlie. He clenched his jaw at the thought.

Harry remembered the way she'd looked at him when he'd surprised her in the morgue. Shock and wariness, combined with that slow, casual appraisal she'd given him before turning back to the cadaver. The desire he'd known to be steadily building for this intriguing woman had doubled in that instant.

Harry walked down the corridor towards his apartment, being as quiet as he could, mindful of the early morning hour and his elderly neighbours. When he was inside, he switched on the air-conditioning, dumped his briefcase in the study and headed straight for the shower. His body was exhausted, even though his mind seemed to be jumping from one thought to another.

The water was soothing on his shoulders. What he wouldn't give for a massage…a massage from Kimberlie Mason? He closed his eyes, dismissing the thought as soon as it entered his mind. She was his colleague—and a junior one at that. She would be working in his department for a few months and then she'd be moving on to the next aspect of her training, which would be at the children's hospital.

Turning the taps off, he towelled himself dry and pulled on a pair of boxer shorts which had cartoon characters on them. He brushed his teeth and lay down on his bed, reaching for the latest medical journal from his bedside table. It was the usual way he unwound so he could sleep, but tonight it wasn't working. A red-headed service registrar with a pair of amazing green eyes was disturbing his thoughts.

He tossed the journal aside, switched off the light and laced his fingers behind his head, deciding to let the thoughts flow. They'd been threatening at the back of his mind all week long and tonight it was either risk a pounding headache or fantasise what it would be like to take her in his arms and press his lips to hers—because that was exactly what he wanted to do to the alluring Dr Mason.

CHAPTER THREE

'PSSST.'

Harry was just coming back from his early morning run. After two hours of tossing and turning, he'd eventually given up any pretence of resting and had gone for a run to release the tension in his body.

It was almost seven o'clock and he wondered if he could now get a few hours sleep before heading to the hospital.

'Pssst.'

There was that noise again. He stopped and looked around before heading over to Mrs Pressman's door, which was slightly ajar. He could only see half of her face as she peered out through the gap between the safety chain and the doorframe. 'Hi,' Harry said softly. 'How's the leg?'

'Better,' she whispered. 'The district nurse is coming around again today so I'm doing my exercises.'

'Don't forget to rest, Mrs Pressman. Leg ulcers are not to be treated lightly.'

'I know that.' She waved away his concern. 'If you'll be quiet for two seconds and listen to me…' She tut-tutted, not finishing her sentence. 'There's someone in your apartment,' she told him in a conspiratorial whisper.

Harry was immediately alert. Yesterday had been a crazy day with what had happened to Mr Japarlin and the discussion he'd had with Kimberlie about murder. Now someone was poking around in his apartment? 'Are you sure?'

'I saw her go in.'

At the 'her' from Mrs Pressman, Harry relaxed a little. 'Have you seen her before?'

'I think it's that horrible woman you dated last year when your brain wasn't working properly.'

'Thank you,' he said drolly.

'Her hair's different but she came up with Clarry, the new guard, about ten minutes ago. Said she was your fiancée.'

'Did she, now? Well, I'm sure it's nothing to worry about. Thanks for the tip, Mrs Pressman. Now, go and rest that leg.' He smiled sweetly at the elderly woman who looked upon him as another of her sons.

'Yes, Doctor.' She giggled before closing her door.

He could always rely on Mrs Pressman if anything out of the ordinary was happening on the third floor of this apartment building. In fact, she had a good grasp of what was going on in the entire building.

Harry took a deep breath before turning the doorhandle. It was unlocked. The curtains were open and sunlight was flooding the room.

'Hi, honey, I'm home,' he called, his tone bland as he shut the door behind him. 'Elaine, you might as well come out because I know you're here.'

A second later, Elaine Parkinson, the hospital investigation co-ordinator, appeared in the doorway to his kitchen. She was once again dressed immaculately in one of her power suits, her hair tied up in the same professional knot.

'Going to work?'

'I've just put the kettle on,' she crooned, ignoring his question. 'Coffee?' Then she brought the coffee-stained shirt out from behind her back—the one he'd stripped off and left lying on the lounge room floor yesterday afternoon in the rush to change his clothes before heading back to the hospital. 'Oh, I see you've already had some.' Elaine sniggered and Harry groaned.

'You're trespassing. I could have you arrested for being here.'

'But you won't,' Elaine said sweetly. 'Not an old...*friend*.' She dropped the shirt to the floor and stepped on it as she walked towards him. 'Although I am surprised you didn't change the code on your security alarm. But now I come to think about it, perhaps you didn't because you knew I'd be back for more.'

'I didn't think you'd stoop to breaking and entering. Besides, whatever happened between us, Elaine, is *over*.'

Elaine dropped the seductive pretence for a moment. 'I suppose your little spying neighbour told you I was here.'

Harry didn't reply but glared at her for a moment. 'What do you want?' He was tired and not in the mood for any of Elaine's games.

'You're such an attractive man, Harry. It's a pity we couldn't work out our differences.'

'The main one being I believe in truthful, monogamous relationships.'

Elaine waved away his words. 'So traditional of you, darling. I wish you'd get over what that little wife of yours did to you. For centuries, men have always enjoyed…shall we say *variety* when it comes to women, so why can't a woman do the same to men?'

Harry looked at her in complete disgust. Now his blinkers were off where Elaine was concerned, he wondered what had happened to his judgement last year, when they'd dated for just under six months. She was damaged goods.

'Let's be adult about this,' she purred in a way she clearly thought was seductive. 'I want you…you want me.' She reached out and stroked one perfectly manicured finger down the side of his cheek.

Harry caught her wrist and firmly removed her hand from his face. 'That's where you're wrong. I don't want you, Elaine, and for your information I am not even remotely attracted to you any more.' Still holding her arm, he marched her over to the door and opened it. 'Get out.' Once she was through the doorway, he shut her out and locked the door.

He headed into the kitchen for a cup of coffee, picking up his shirt as he went. He hadn't had time to do anything other than change before heading back to the hospital the previous evening, as he'd been eager to get to the morgue to view Mr Japarlin's body, and last night he'd completely forgotten about the stained shirt.

He set it to soak, poured himself a glass of orange juice while he waited for the kettle to boil and sat down to rest. A moment later his mind was once again sorting through the problems he'd pigeonholed during his run and now the one Elaine had added to the list.

She was wrong in one respect. He *had* come to terms with what had happened between himself and his wife. After all, it had been almost ten years since he'd had their marriage annulled. The pain wasn't there any more but the caution was. It was a caution he lived by where women were concerned, and if there were things which didn't add up, he had learned to confront rather than blindly accept. It was what he'd done with Elaine and had been proved right when she'd admitted to seeing other men.

But what of Kimberlie? She'd turned up in his operating room for the first time and a patient had died on the table. He still wasn't sure what could possibly have gone wrong, and at the morgue he'd been relieved to discover nothing untoward with the deceased. It confirmed *he* hadn't done anything incorrectly while operating.

Harry had also been surprised to find his service registrar there. He sat back in his chair and breathed deeply. Kimberlie Mason. When he'd signed in with the morgue security guard, he'd been told no one was back with the cadavers, except for a cleaner who was finishing up late.

So why had she been there? What had she been looking for? What had happened to the theatre bins? Did she know anything about them? It didn't add up. Nothing added up, and that fact alone bothered him to the point of annoyance.

Could he question her about this? Was it really his business? If they were involved in a relationship and strange things were happening, he'd be asking and demanding answers, but this was different. This wasn't romantic. Sure, he was attracted to Kimberlie but, where Mr Japarlin's death was concerned, it was a moot point.

With everything that had happened yesterday, he had a million and one unanswered questions and most of them concerned Dr Mason. He made the decision to keep a closer eye on her than normal…and he was looking forward to the prospect.

'Oh, this is ridiculous,' Kim said out loud as she stood from her cross-legged position on the floor. With her foot half-asleep and tingling with pins and needles, she limped to the kitchen, being careful not to disturb the spread of papers she was desperately trying to make sense of.

Pouring herself a nice cool drink, she returned and looked down at the different dossiers she'd been given for the staff at Sydney General hospital. There were several Tarparniians working at the hospital and, of course, other staff, like

Harry, who were in some way connected with the country.

The minister's death had been on the late news. It had been announced he'd died of natural causes but a full investigation would be undertaken. She'd contacted Ivan in the morgue who'd told her the autopsy was set for Monday morning.

Kim looked at the picture of Harry Buchanan once more and shook her head. 'You're getting too close, Kimmy. You need to be professional, keep your distance and get the job done. No time to waste over the likes of tall, dark and handsome Dr Buchanan.'

To prove she meant business, she relegated his photo and dossier to the bottom of her pile and focused her attention on the next one.

Theatre nurse Ni Kartu. Kim had already discovered he was passionate about what was happening in his home land of Tarparnii but was that enough to drive him to commit murder?

John McPhee, the anaesthetist for Mr Japarlin's operation, was the head of anaesthetics. He'd been married for almost ten years, no children and lived a life of luxury. His wife, Kat, was a New Zealander. Kim stared hard at John's photograph. She hadn't spoken to him as he tended to thumb his nose at doctors in her lowly position but, just from looking at him, he had the eyes of a confused man.

A knock at the door made her jump and spill her drink. She quickly got to her feet, brushing the wetness from the comfortable T-shirt and shorts she was wearing. She checked the peep-hole and smiled as she opened the door for Tammy.

Tammy looked at Kim's top. 'Startle you again?'

Kim laughed and shook her head in dismay. 'You'd think I'd have nerves of steel, but when I'm deep in concentration mode anything can startle me.'

'Don't mention that to Moss.' Tammy shut the door behind her. She held out a paper bag to Kim. 'Chocolate-chip muffins. Cooked fresh from your favourite bakery.'

Kim accepted the bag and gave her friend a hug. 'You're the best, Tam. How did you know?'

'You never eat breakfast unless it's after mid-day—especially if it's a Saturday morning and you don't have to work.'

'You're right again. Help yourself to a drink and then help me make sense of what's going on at that hospital.'

While Kim waited for Tammy, she snuck the picture of Harry out from the bottom of the pile and sat cross-legged on the comfortable sofa to stare into his hypnotic eyes. Even though the picture was two-dimensional, there was still an unreadable depth in his gaze and from the start it had intrigued her. Now that she'd met him, been in close proximity with him, felt an overwhelming tug of desire towards him, she was more interested in finding out what made Harry Buchanan tick.

'Here's your muffin, Kim.'

Kim jumped again, Harry's picture flying from her hands as she knocked the muffin from the plate Tammy had been holding out to her.

'Man, you *do* have it bad.' Tammy snatched up the photo before Kim could, leaving her to pick up the muffin. 'Mmm-*mmm*. What a dish. You know, with a man like Harry Buchanan around, there may be the slightest chance you could get…hmm…' Tammy put her head on the side and looked thoughtfully at her friend. 'A little distracted?'

'Well… I…er—'

'Nah. Not the great Kimberlie Mason, super-spy extraordinaire!'

'I'm *not* a super-spy. I'm a government operative on loan from—'

'On loan from the army,' Tammy interrupted. 'I know, I know.' She grinned at her friend and glanced down at the picture. 'So, Major?' Tammy settled herself on the opposite side of the sofa, her eyes alight with eagerness. 'What's he like? Is he as good-looking in person as he is in this picture?'

'Better.' Kim sighed and smiled at her friend. Both of them giggled. They'd known each other since kindergarten and it had been Tammy who had unwittingly led Kim into the Australian Secret Intelligence Service. Always the adventurous one, Tammy had jet-setted around the world for a few years after finishing school, enjoying extreme sports, but after breaking almost every bone in her body, she'd come back home and settled down…well, settled down more than before.

When Kim's parents hadn't had the money to pay for her to go to medical school, it had been Tammy who'd suggested Kim join the army. The army had paid for Kim's training and in return Kim had worked for them. That had been, until five years ago when she'd been seconded by ASIS for a medical mission. Then another one had come up and then another. Now she felt as though she worked more for ASIS than she did for the army.

They knew each other so well there was no way Kim could hide anything from Tammy.

Neither did she want to, and her smile increased as they both stared at the picture of Harry. 'He's so sweet.'

'Sweet?' Tammy was surprised. 'Sweet? That wouldn't have been the first adjective I'd have thought of to describe him.'

'No. He's direct, stubborn, authoritative—'

'Hot, sexy and delicious,' Tammy added.

'And sweet.'

'You got all that in one week?'

Kim looked at the photo for a moment longer before putting it face down on the table. 'I got more than that. He's going to be a problem if I'm not careful.'

Tammy shrugged. 'You're a professional. You'll deal with it.'

'That's right. I will. But the main thing I wanted you to know is that Harry wants to look into Japarlin's death. He doesn't think it was an accident either. He caught me in the morgue. He came in and together we looked at the body and then returned to his office, where he agreed there were suspicious circumstances surrounding the patient.'

'Why is he so gung-ho about this?'

'Because he's never had a patient die on the table before. I think at first he didn't want to admit it could happen to him, but the more he thought about it, the more he realised it wasn't logical, not in this instance anyway. Japarlin wasn't a high-risk patient and a mysterious myocardial infarction was too much of a coincidence for Harry to accept.'

'Do you think he had anything to do with it? Is he using you to cover his own tracks? You know, confiding in you to help hide the truth?'

'He could be but…' she shrugged '…my instincts tell me he's on the level. He has too much concern, and wouldn't he be trying to put my mind at ease instead of suggesting we investigate the death together?'

'First rule of espionage—consider everything a trap.'

'You're right.' Kim nodded.

'Besides, Moss wants him…' Tammy paused and raised her eyebrows suggestively. 'Thoroughly checked out!'

Kim laughed.

'Hey, that's a direct order, Major.'

'Yes, ma'am. I'll take a look around his apartment. Do I need to bug it?'

'Not at this stage, but a word of caution—make sure you do it when he's not there or at least when he's asleep.'

'Tammy!' Kim's jaw dropped open in shock. 'I'm not that kind of girl.'

'No. You're a spy. Look for communiqués, faxes, and get a copy of his hard drive. When will you do it?'

'There's a function on at the hospital tonight he's supposed to attend so I thought that would be perfect.'

'Yep. I'll organise a surveillance van and be outside to render assistance.' Tammy grinned. 'Just in case he comes home early and you need help tying him up.'

'Tamara!' Kim threw a cushion at her friend and they both laughed. 'I'm getting all hot and flustered.'

Tammy's grin faded and she looked more closely at her friend. 'You really like him,' she stated.

'Well, for now I do. Let's see if he's clean first.'

'Right. I'll have someone check the water meter—see how often he showers.'

Another cushion made its way over the room to collide with Tammy's face. Her friend laughed. 'At least I know if a pillow fight breaks out, you'll be well qualified.'

'Stop it,' Kim warned, lifting her last cushion, the smile still on her face.

'OK. OK. I'll stop…for now.'

'Thank you.' Kim picked up the next dossier but paused and slowly looked up at her friend, all humour gone. 'What if Harry's for real? What if he isn't part of this, has stumbled across it unwittingly and ends up in danger?'

'You'll have to monitor that. If you think things are getting out of control, bring him in and we'll place him in protective custody, but that's a last resort.'

Kim nodded. 'What about the bins? Harry noticed they were missing, by the way, so we'll need to fudge the records to keep it all straight.'

'I'll take care of that. Nothing has come up yet but testing is still being done. I'll call anything through the minute we know.'

'Thanks.'

'All right. Let's discuss the other suspects and what to do about them.' Both women worked solidly for the next hour, devouring the muffins and drinking cups of coffee.

Kim stood up gingerly and stretched. As she headed to the bathroom, there was a knock at the door. She stopped and looked at Tammy.

'Expecting someone?' Tammy's voice was soft.

'No.' Kim hurried to the door and checked the peephole. She gasped. 'It's *him*.'

'Who's him?'

'Harry!' Kim flapped her hands in agitation and quickly hurried over to help Tammy gather up the papers strewn all over the coffee-table.

'Go. Go,' Tammy said, and Kim went to the door. She looked down at her baggy clothes and cringed, amazed she was going to let him see her like this. Oh, well. Straightening her shoulders, she quickly fluffed a hand through her curls before opening the door.

'Harry?' She couldn't hide her surprise…and her pleasure. 'Um, what are you doing here?'

It was a good question and one he still didn't know the answer to. All he knew was that he hadn't been able to stop thinking about her. He cleared his throat. 'I have some things I want to discuss with you.'

'Uh… OK.' She glanced over her shoulder to where she hoped Tammy had finished packing up the papers, but there was no sign of her friend, or the files. 'Come in.' She stepped back to allow him to enter before closing the door.

Harry glanced around the apartment and his first thought was that it looked more like a hotel room. It was clean, comfortable and…impersonal. There didn't seem to be any of Kimberlie's natural vibrancy about the place and that surprised him. When another woman walked in from the kitchen, he turned to face Kimberlie. 'I'm sorry. I didn't realise you had company.'

'Huh?' Kim stared at him for a moment, still unable to believe he was standing in her apartment. Then she saw Tammy and quickly recovered. 'Oh, uh…Harry, this is my friend Tammy.'

Tammy smiled and shook his hand. 'I understand you're Kim's new boss?'

'Yes. Although Kimberlie's only been at the hospital for one week, it's been…' He paused and turned to look at his service registrar. 'Quite a week.'

'I'm sure.'

'Please, have a seat,' Kim offered. 'Can I get you a drink? Tea? Coffee?'

Harry's smile was immediate. 'Coffee would be nice, but are you sure it's safe?'

'Safe?' Tammy asked, looking from her friend back to their guest as though she were at a tennis match.

Kim groaned with embarrassment. 'I'll put the coffee on,' she said, and quickly exited stage left. She emptied out the stewed coffee and set the coffee-machine up again. Next, she made a rapid but necessary pit stop to the bathroom and winced as she caught sight of her reflection. It was too late to change now, too late to put on some lipstick and do more than finger-comb her hair. It would give too much away, make her look like she was trying too hard, which was ludicrous because Harry was nothing more than a colleague—a colleague she needed to investigate. She heard Tammy laughing and knew he'd told the story about how she'd dumped coffee on him yesterday.

She returned to the kitchen, opened the cupboard and found the dossier files stuffed on top of the cups. 'Good one, Tam,' she muttered.

'Can I help?'

At the sound of Harry's voice, Kim quickly grabbed a cup, shut the cupboard and turned to face him. 'No. No. Everything's fine. Why don't you go and sit down and I'll bring it in?'

'Tammy's phone rang so I thought I'd give her a bit of privacy.'

'Oh.' Kim smiled before forcing herself to move. She glanced at the coffee-machine, willing it to drip faster. 'Er… milk? Sugar?'

'Two sugars, thanks. No milk.'

There was silence as she put sugar into his cup.

'You're not having one?' he queried.

'My cup's in the other room. I'll get it when Tammy's finished on the phone.' The silence stretched once more. Kim searched wildly for a neutral topic but all she could think of was that

Harry was here, standing opposite her in her kitchen. He was dressed in jeans and a polo shirt and as her gaze travelled over his long legs, noticing the way the fabric pulled tighter around his quads, then up to his broad shoulders, it was all she could do not to sigh with longing.

'Shall I turn?' His voice deep with amusement.

'Oh!' She gasped and covered her face with her hands. 'I'm sorry.'

'Don't be. I enjoyed it.'

'Harry!'

'What?'

'Stop. You're embarrassing me.'

'I think you're doing a fine job of that all by yourself, Dr Mason.'

Kim looked down at her hands and forced herself to take a deep breath. She glanced up at Harry again, deciding it was time she took control of the situation. 'Why did you drop around and, incidentally, how did you know which apartment?'

'It's in your personnel file.'

'Which you just happened to get a look at, I suppose.'

'Obviously.'

'Hmm. So, anyway, you came around because…?'

'I have to attend a head-of-unit dinner tonight and I was wondering if you'd like to come with me.'

'But I'm not head of a unit.'

He smiled. 'I meant as my date.'

'Oh.' Wow! She could hardly believe he was asking her out. She hadn't been asked out in such a long time. As her job required her to move around quite a bit, she didn't have enough opportunities to meet good-looking, single men and now that she had, not only was he her superior at the hospital but he was also a suspect. It wasn't fair. It just wasn't fair.

'I can see I've shocked you completely.'

'Wouldn't tongues wag if we went together? I mean, in my experience hospital grapevines are always looking for something new to latch onto.'

'That honestly doesn't bother me. Would it bother you?'

'Uh…no.' She wouldn't be bothered with the gossip about herself, but she'd found that it was an interesting way to pick up leads in the cases she worked on. If people were to start gossiping about her, they'd probably stop talking when she came into the room. That wouldn't bother her emotionally but it would professionally. She had a job to do and she needed to remain focused.

Besides, she needed to get into Harry's apartment.

'So you'll come.' It was a statement and Kim quickly shook her head.

'I'm sorry, Harry. I can't. I need to study.' After all, it was what service registrars did.

'Sure you can't take a night off?'

Kim laughed. 'You've obviously forgotten what it was like, being bottom of the ladder. I need to study.' He didn't need to know *what* she was planning on studying. Thankfully, the coffee was ready so she poured him a cup and stirred in the sugar before handing him the cup.

'There's no way I can change your mind?' He took a sip.

She shook her head. 'Sorry. If you need to take a date, you've left it a bit late.' She shrugged, feeling mischievous. 'You could take Tammy.'

'I've only just met Tammy. I don't know anything about her.'

'You don't know anything about me either.'

'I know more about you than I do about her.'

'Really?' Kim's smile increased. 'Like what?'

He slowly raised the cup to his lips, sipping quietly from the hot liquid, his gaze never leaving hers. He returned the cup to the bench and swallowed. 'I know you're good at your job, you can pre-empt well in Theatre, which will stand you in good stead for the future.' He shifted his weight and she could have sworn he moved a little closer.

'You're right-handed, currently don't own a car and get annoyed with your curls when they come loose from the band.' He edged closer still and Kim held her breath, his deep tone washing over her, hypnotising her. He reached out and gently touched her hair before tucking a few of the wayward curls behind her ear. 'Your green eyes flash like emeralds shining in the sun whenever you're cross, frustrated, and especially when your senses are…heightened.'

He moved closer still and she could now feel his breath caressing her cheek. 'You feel the awareness between us, this natural attraction. Neither of us asked for it but it's there.' His fingers caressed her cheek and as he tenderly ran his thumb over her lips, Kim gasped with longing.

There was no way she could move, even if she'd wanted to. He'd caught her in his snare and she'd never felt so wonderfully helpless in her life.

'Kimberlie.'

The way he whispered her name, the way it was filled with such longing and need, caused goose-bumps to tingle down her spine.

'Is that coffee ready yet?' Tammy asked, coming through into the kitchen.

Kim and Harry both instantly took a step backwards.

'Whoops. Sorry,' Tammy added, before doing a U-turn and leaving them alone.

Kim was astounded at what had almost happened. Harry had almost kissed her! This time the emotions had been more powerful, more potent, and definitely more personal than the previous moment they'd shared in his office yesterday.

Harry swallowed. 'I'd better go.'

She didn't try and stop him. On wooden legs, she walked him to the door and after throwing a 'goodbye' in Tammy's direction, he paused and looked at Kim again before nodding briskly and leaving.

'Well, if that wasn't a moment to beat all. Sorry I walked in when I did.'

'No. No. Thank you for walking in when you did.' Kim hit her head with her hand. 'What was I thinking?'

'You weren't, and that's not such a bad thing.'

'What? Have you completely taken leave of your senses? The man's a suspect!' She gestured towards the door he'd just left by, before hitting herself in the head once more. 'Stupid, stupid, stupid.'

Tammy walked over and led her to the sofa. 'Sit down. It's not stupid. He's a good-looking, single man who is interested in you. What's wrong with that?'

'Tammy!'

'You need to get over Chris.'

'I'm over Chris.'

'Really?'

'Yes. I'm not over how stupid Chris was and that in our line of work we flirt with death more frequently than normal people.'

'Which means what? You want to be a normal person again?'

Kim frowned. 'I don't know. I listen to my mum, telling me to settle down, to have a family, that I'm thirty-two and the biological clock is ticking, and you know what, Tam? She's right. I'm attracted to Harry but what if my job ends up hurting him? What if he ends up in the line of fire, so to speak? I was responsible for Chris and look what happened to him.'

'Chris was different. He didn't follow orders. He didn't listen.'

Kim brushed the thoughts away with her hand. 'No. I'm just going to focus on my job and that's it. No more "moments" with Harry.'

'Right, so go to his place tonight, look for evidence to prove one way or another if he's involved. If your gut instinct is right—which it usually is—Harry's in the clear and *then* you'll have the problem of deciding what to do.'

'And the part about me being a government operative? How or even *when* do I tell him about that? Or the fact that I'm lying to him, not only about my qualifications but everything else?'

Tammy shrugged. 'No relationship is perfect.'

'He's been burned before.' She gestured to the kitchen where the dossiers were. 'He was married and so was his wife…to another man! That must have destroyed him. Even the nurses at the hospital have already warned me against ever lying to Harry, and here I am *living* a lie every second we're together.'

'It's your job,' Tammy pointed out logically.

Kim groaned and buried her face in her hands. 'I know, but he's so cute.'

'Yes, he is.' Tammy patted her friend's back. 'Tell you what. How about we go down to head office and beat up on the martial arts dummies?'

'That's not a nice way to talk about Moss,' Kim retorted, and they both laughed, the tension easing.

'There you go. Happy again, and I won't even tell Moss you think he's a dummy.'

'Thanks. Never a good thing to call your superior,' Kim agreed, forcing her thoughts to stay well away from her other 'superior'.

Just after half past eight that evening, Kim picked the lock on Harry's apartment door. She should have taken her gloves off. It was much easier to pick locks without the added obstacle of gloves. 'Come on, come on,' she whispered as she heard the lift bell chime. *'Yes.'* She pushed open the door and slipped inside, narrowly missing being seen. She hooked a small decoding device to Harry's security alarm and within seconds it had accessed the code. Kim slipped the device into one of the pockets on her ankle-length black coat.

'I'm in,' she said softly, knowing the subvocal earpiece she was wearing would pick up her words.

'Good. Head for his study.' Tammy's voice came through her earpiece as Kim pulled a torch from one of her many pockets. Dressed similarly to the night before, in dark clothes, she shone the light around the room. She was surprised to see a few pieces of clothing lying on the floor, and when she took a closer look she realised they were the clothes he'd been wearing that day. For some reason she'd expected him to be immaculate in everything he did. It was nice to see he *was* human in this small and personal way.

Her fingers itched to pick the clothes up, to fold them, but she resisted. She wasn't here to clean his apartment.

Moving from room to room, she found his study. 'OK. Let's see what we've got.'

'Psst,' came the familiar sound from his neighbour's doorway.

'Evening, Mrs Pressman. How's the leg?'

'She's back again,' Mrs Pressman said, not answering his question and pointing her finger to his door.

'Really?' he groaned. 'That's the last thing I need tonight.'

'I was getting out of the lift when I saw something dark—like a woman's dress—go into your apartment. I called down to Clarry but he said he hadn't brought anyone up. Not after the talking-to he'd been given by his boss. So, anyway, I told him to tell me when you arrived so I wouldn't miss you.'

'Thanks, Mrs Pressman. I'll deal with her. Now, you really should be off that leg.'

'Yes, Doctor.' Mrs Pressman giggled.

'Goodnight,' he said caringly. He walked over to his door and tried the handle. It was locked.

Elaine hadn't locked it last night. He opened the door and called, 'Hi, honey. I'm home—again.' His tone was more bland, more bored than it had been previously. He made a mental note to change the code on his security alarm as soon as Elaine left.

'Come on, Elaine,' he called as he switched on the light. 'I know you're here.' Harry walked through to the kitchen and switched that light on, too. 'Mrs Pressman, my pesky neighbour, saw you come in again.'

Kim worked hard to keep her heart rate under control as she closed the final drawer of his filing cabinet. When Tammy's urgent call had come through that Harry was entering the building, Kim had quickly started clearing up, hoping to slip out before he arrived. No such luck.

Why did he think Elaine was here? Kim didn't bother to try and figure it out now. All she wanted to do was escape. She crossed to the door and stood behind it, just in case he opened it.

'Elaine, I'm not in the mood for your silly games,' he called, and she could tell he must be somewhere in the front rooms of his apartment.

Keeping calm and trying to ignore the knots in her stomach, she edged out into the hallway. She'd been in situations like this before and had always managed to escape, but this was no ordinary situation. She knew this man, she liked this man, and for him to find her snooping in his apartment wasn't a particularly good way to get him to ask her out on another date.

He was switching lights on left, right and centre. She saw him head towards his bedroom, the scowl on his face indicating he wasn't too impressed with what was going on.

Now was her chance. She slid along the wall, keeping in the shadows as best she could. Deciding to use the situation to her best advantage, Kim switched out the kitchen light and sprinted quietly towards the front door. The hall was bathed in light but she managed to turn the switch off, plunging it back into darkness just as he rounded the corner of the kitchen.

'Cut it out, Elaine. Your sick and pathetic games are wasted on me.'

Kim stood flush with the wall as she slowly inched towards the front door. She was almost there. Reaching out, she placed her hand on the doorknob and started to turn it.

He was silent and for a moment she wasn't too sure where he was.

'Gotcha!' he said triumphantly.

CHAPTER FOUR

KIM felt the hand on her shoulder and reacted instantly.

She swung around, her elbow raised to break the hold. It connected with Harry's jaw and he staggered backwards. She opened the door, desperate to get out, and he lunged at her once more. He slammed her up against the wall, his shoulder in her stomach, and she groaned, surprised. She was impressed he was putting up a fight. Grabbing a handful of his hair, she jerked his head backwards and he yelled in pain.

The sound tore through her, crushing her, but Tammy's voice of reason was telling her to get out of there, and fast. With adrenaline pumping, Kim swung around, her foot connecting with his solar plexus before she elbowed him across the back of his neck.

He slumped to the ground—motionless.

Kim stared down at his dark form, knowing she should be moving but unable to do so.

'Get out of there,' Tammy's voice said once more.

'I've knocked him unconscious,' she whispered in dismay.

'Get out,' Tammy stated. 'That's an order, Kim.'

There was nothing left for her to do but leave. She glanced down at him once more as she locked the door from the inside before pulling it shut. She ripped off her beanie and shoved it into one of her coat pockets before taking off the coat and rolling it up as she headed for the stairwell. When she arrived at the surveillance van across the street, she threw her coat in and yanked off her gloves.

'I'm going back.' She pulled out her earpiece and handed it to Tammy. 'As I reported to you earlier, I couldn't find anything in his apartment to suggest he was involved in the minister's death, but it wouldn't hurt for me to take another look around.'

'Now?' Tammy was shocked.

'Perhaps. My main motive for going back now is to check on him.'

'And what will be your cover for being there?'

Kim reached over into the front passenger seat and pulled out a shopping bag. 'I bought him a new shirt to replace the one I spilt coffee over.'

Tammy smiled. 'Good thinking. All right. Go check on him.'

'OK. First, switch tops with me.' Kim pulled off her black long-sleeved top and swapped it for Tammy's red V-neck. 'Thanks.'

'Put the earpiece back in, though.' Tammy held it out to her. 'Just in case.'

Kim did as she was asked and, with the shopping bag in hand, crossed the street, pulling the band out of her hair as she went, sending her curls cascading down around her shoulders. This time she checked in with Security, and when Clarry, the guard on duty, couldn't get through to Harry, he left his partner in charge of the desk and walked with Kim up to Harry's apartment.

'Dr Buchanan?' he called as he knocked on the door.

'Psst. Clarry?'

The sound came from a few doors down and Kim turned to see a woman peeking out from behind her door chain.

'Not now, Mrs Pressman.' Clarry knocked again and jangled his keyring, finding the master key. 'Dr Buchanan? Is everything all right?'

'He might be in the shower,' Kim volunteered.

There was a muffled sound from inside and Kim breathed a sigh of relief. At least he was conscious.

'Dr Buchanan, I'm coming in,' Clarry called, and unlocked the door. Another groan of pain met them as the security guard quickly switched on the light. 'Dr Buchanan!'

'Harry!' Kim dumped her shopping bag and rushed to his side. 'What happened? Are you all right?'

'Must have tripped,' he muttered, as he allowed Kim to help him to the lounge.

'Do you need a doctor?'

'I *am* a doctor,' Kim said. 'Don't worry, Clarry. Thanks for letting me in. I'll take care of him.' Kim stood and walked him to the door. 'I think Dr Buchanan would like a little privacy. He may feel a little…well, you know… embarrassed at all this fuss.'

'Oh, yes.' Clarry nodded.

'Go and put Mrs Pressman's mind at rest.'

'Will do. Goodnight, Dr Mason.'

With Clarry out of the way, Kim crossed to Harry's side. 'I'm OK,' he muttered.

'You're not. Let me take a look at you.'

'I'm fine.'

'Harry!' She lifted his head to look at him and was instantly swamped with guilt at the red lump appearing above his right eyebrow where she'd elbowed him. 'Ooh. Nice bump there.'

He rubbed the back of his neck and she pushed his hand away. 'And another one here. Harry, these injuries don't happen when you fall down.'

'I didn't fall down,' he muttered. 'I just said that to get rid of Clarry. Someone attacked me.'

Kim found it hard to speak. His voice was filled with loathing, self-disgust and indignation. She swallowed and knew she had to get it together. 'I'll get you an ice pack and some paracetamol.' She spoke softly, and quickly went into the kitchen. 'I feel so guilty,' she whispered, but knew Tammy would hear her. After opening several cupboards she finally found a medical kit. She found two ice packs in the freezer, wrapped them in tea-towels and poured him a glass of water. She carried everything back into the lounge room.

'Take these,' she ordered, handing him two paracetamol tablets, and was glad when he obliged. She placed the ice packs on his head and neck and made him lie down with his feet elevated.

'I'm fine, Kimberlie.'

'Do as you're told, Doctor.' Thankfully, he did. 'Someone attacked you?'

'I feel so stupid.'

'Why?' She sat on the edge of the lounge beside him.

'Because I didn't stop him.'

'Good,' Tammy said. 'He thinks the attacker was male.'

'I don't think you should blame yourself for that. Was the door open when you got home?' She reached into the medical kit and found his penlight. She checked his pupils. 'Equal and reacting to light,' she stated.

'No. The door was locked.'

Kim hooked the stethoscope into her ears and listened to his chest. 'Breathing is normal.' She felt his head. 'You don't feel hot or clammy. That's a good sign.' She pulled out his portable sphygmomanometer and wound the cuff round his arm. 'Keep going. Tell me what happened.'

'I came home from the dinner early because it was so boring—especially as you refused to accompany me.'

'Oh, so this is all my fault.' Never a truer word had she spoken.

He smiled and she was glad to see his mental clarity seemed fine. 'Most certainly. If you'd come with me, I wouldn't have wanted to come home early.'

'So, anyway, you came home from the dinner early and…?' She hooked the stethoscope into her ears again and pumped up the cuff.

'And the door was locked. The alarm had been turned off and for a moment I thought it was…' He stopped and glanced at her. 'I thought it was Elaine.'

'Elaine?' Kim concentrated on the BP reading before releasing the pressure. 'BP's normal.'

'Elaine Parkinson—administrator from the hospital. We dated last year but it's over.'

'Does she know this?' She packed the sphygmo away.

'Yes. She stopped by my apartment yesterday morning, which was why I thought it was her again tonight.'

'Well, that covers that question,' Tammy said, and Kim almost jumped at hearing her friend's voice.

'But it wasn't,' Kim stated.

'No.'

'Do you know who it was?'

'No.'

'Why would someone break in? Do you know?' She watched him closely to see if he was lying when he answered.

'No.'

He hadn't faltered and she believed him. 'Burglar?'

'Sophisticated one, as the door was locked and the alarm was off.'

'Let me get the phone and call the police.' She started to move but he reached out to stop her.

'No. It's all right.'

'Are you sure? Harry, it's not every day someone breaks into your apartment and then hurts you. This is serious.' Again she watched him for a reaction but he merely closed his eyes. 'Harry? Are you sure you don't know why someone would break in?'

He exhaled harshly and winced in pain. Kim winced in sympathy. 'The only strange thing which has happened to me lately has been…' He opened his eyes and met her gaze. 'Mr Japarlin's death.'

Her eyes widened. 'You think the break-in was something to do with that?'

'Oh, he's good,' Tammy said in her ear.

'I don't know.'

'Do you want me to see if anything's missing?' She glanced around his apartment, instantly grinning at the clothes on the floor. 'Apart from a cleaning lady, that is.'

Harry smiled. 'So I'm not that tidy. Don't bother looking. How would you know if anything was missing?'

'Good point, but I was just trying to be helpful.'

Harry took her hand in his. 'You *are* being helpful. In fact, I could get used to being nursed by you.'

'Really?'

He frowned. 'Why are *you* here? It's late. I hope you took a taxi to come here instead of the train.'

Kim couldn't help but smile at his concern for her welfare, especially when she was the one who was responsible for his present condition.

'Tammy dropped me off on her way home.'

He nodded slowly. 'So she doesn't live with you, then?'

'No.'

'You live alone.'

'Yes.'

'Something else we have in common.'

'Dr Buchanan, you're flirting with me.'

'So?'

'So how am I supposed to know if it's real or just a delusion you're under because you've sustained a blow to the head?'

'You're just going to have to chance it.' His voice was a whisper as he reached out his hand to caress her cheek. Kim couldn't have moved even if she'd wanted to. There he was, lying back on the lounge, his head propped up on one pillow, his feet up on three, ice packs here and there where bruises would already be forming, and she thought he'd never looked more sexy.

It was his eyes, she realised. Those 'come hither' eyes—bedroom eyes. The blue depths were dark with repressed desire, which made the world around them disappear, leaving just the two of them, their emotions and feelings the only things that mattered. The warmth of his hand on her face, the way his thumb was once more tracing over her lips as it had done earlier that morning was enough to cause a fire to spread throughout her entire body.

No man had ever affected her this way before. Harry was definitely one of a kind and Kim could feel herself being drawn closer to him by some strange and mysterious invisible cord. It was as though he'd lassoed her and was hauling her in, but Harry was no cowboy. He was a brilliant surgeon, one whom she admired and had great respect for, yet at the moment he was a man evoking such havoc in her senses she doubted she'd ever recover.

'I…um…bought you a new shirt,' she stammered, inclining her head towards where the shopping bag lay but never once breaking eye contact with him. 'I felt guilty about spilling coffee on the other one.'

'That's nice.' She was mesmerised with the way his lips moved even though she had no idea what he'd just said.

'Hmm?'

'Kimberlie. I need to kiss you.'

Her breathing, which she hadn't thought could get any faster, increased at his words. Her heart was pounding furiously in her chest, the blood pumping wildly around her body, and she knew she needed to kiss him just as much.

He urged her down, closer and closer still, yet when her chest pressed against his, he winced with pain.

Kim grimaced, guilt swamping her once more. 'I'm sorry I hurt you.' The words were a confession but Harry brushed them away and she realised he hadn't picked up on her slip.

He cupped her face in his hands and shifted slightly so she didn't need to lean on his chest. 'You'll hurt me more if you don't kiss me.'

Her smile was slow and deliberate, her words soft. 'Well, we wouldn't want that, now, would we?'

Her tongue slipped between her lips to wet them in anticipation and he groaned, urging her head down so their mouths could finally meet. She gasped with delight at the contact and then sighed into the kiss, her eyelids fluttering closed as a delicious warmth spread through her. Slowly they explored each other, tantalising and tasting. The tip of his tongue traced the outline of her lips, parting them before he claimed access once more.

It was a dance, like the tango, a dance of love and romance, and they were extremely compatible as partners. Feelings of longing swept through her as his masterful mouth continued to set off different sensations—longings to never have this moment end, longings to tell him the truth and longings to stay in his arms for ever.

The warmth of his hands only added to the fire which was burning inside her, and when he sifted his fingers through her curls, gently touching them, she felt a new level of awareness course throughout her. What was it about this man that had her in such a spin? He was good-looking, charming, sweet and an incredible kisser, yet she sensed there was a part of him still holding back. It was their first kiss after all, and she didn't expect him to lay everything on the line, but instinct told her there was much more to this man than he was letting her see…and she was one hundred per cent hooked.

He shifted slightly from his position on the lounge, making more room for her. She was half sitting, half lying and conscious of his injuries, but all she wanted was to stretch out beside him and stay there for ever. The feelings of permanency she was experiencing stunned her yet there was no way she wanted to break contact with the sensual pleasure this man was inflicting on her willing mouth.

Harry's sensations were overwhelming him. Never had any woman ever responded to his kisses the way Kim was. It only fuelled the fire which had been steadily building within him during the past week. He still had a lot of questions but for now everything was shelved as he concentrated on the one thing they both not only wanted but needed—to know each other a *lot* better.

Up until now, he'd kept control of himself, even though it had been difficult at first when she'd responded so ardently to him, but he could feel his restraint about to snap. Plunging his other hand into her soft, silky hair, he deepened the kiss, urging her closer, driving their needs higher and further than he'd ever thought possible. She gasped a little but didn't pull away. Instead, she met his hunger and seemed to relish it. On and on they raged, both of them rising together, until eventually he broke his mouth free to press hot kisses to her face.

Their breathing was ragged and uneven. Kim's body was weak and she was unable to support herself any longer. Carefully, she rested her head on his chest, listening to the pounding of his heart beneath. She took great comfort—and pleasure—in knowing she wasn't the only one affected by the chemistry that existed between them. To know that she had raised Harry to the same heights of desire as he had done for her left her feeling…special.

His arms settled around her and she sighed with contentment.

'You know, Dr Mason,' he said after their pulse rates had begun to return to normal, 'as you were the first medic on the scene, you should really stay for a while and keep a close eye on me. After all, I may be suffering from a concussion.'

Kim smiled in spite of herself. They both knew his injuries weren't that bad but he did have a point.

'You're quite right, Dr Buchanan. It would be wrong of me to leave for a while, especially if you still require further…first aid.' She glanced up at him and he kissed the tip of her nose.

'Just let me hold you for a while,' he said, closing his eyes, and she wasn't about to argue. They stayed like that for about five minutes before Kim slowly raised her head. His breathing had settled to an even rhythm, but even so she prodded him a little to make sure he was still semi-conscious. He moaned and loosened his hold. She took the opportunity to move away and he didn't object.

'I'll go make us a cup of tea,' she whispered near his ear, and again he moaned in response. She smiled and headed through to the kitchen, this time giving in to the urge to pick his clothes up off the floor and toss them on a nearby chair.

She filled the kettle and switched it on before checking on Harry once more. His breathing was still steady and relaxed. She walked quickly through to the study.

'He's asleep,' she said to Tammy.

'And about time, too! Have fun?'

Kim groaned softly. 'I'm so glad you're my partner on this. Anyone else and I might actually be embarrassed.'

'You're embarrassed. I can hear it in your voice,' Tammy teased. 'Is he a good kisser?'

'And then some.'

'OK. I want all the details, but later. Time to get back to work, Kimmy. Are you in the study?'

'Yes, but, as I said before, it's pretty clear. I've looked everywhere here.'

'Try his bedroom.'

'Good thinking.' Kim went down the corridor and stopped on the threshold of his room. 'I can't go in here. What if he wakes and finds me?'

'Throw yourself on the bed and tell him you're glad he's finally come to you.'

Kim giggled. 'Tam!'

'Just get to work. We'll think of something if he comes in.'

She stepped into the room and stared at the large bed which took up most of the space. It was unmade, one pillow was on the floor and his bedside table was strewn with books. She started there, checking each book to make sure nothing fell out. She looked through the bedside-table drawer and beneath the mattress.

'Nothing so far. I'll just go check on him.' He was still asleep, snoring a little, and she returned to his room. The wardrobe didn't take long and as she went through his drawers where he kept his underwear, she had to force herself to keep total control over her wandering thoughts.

'Found anything?' Tammy asked.

'Only that I know he likes to wear boxer shorts.'

Her friend chuckled. 'Anything else?'

'Nope. He's clean.'

'Bathroom? Laundry? Kitchen?'

'I'll get on to those next.' She headed into his bathroom and immediately noticed something out of place. 'He has two mirrors on his bathroom wall.'

'Really?'

Kim crossed to one and opened it, only to find a cupboard containing the usual amenities. She tried the other. 'Bingo.'

'Safe?'

'Yep.'

'Way to go, Kimmy. Can you open it?'

'It's a digital keypad.'

'Cool. Use your decoder.'

'It's in my coat.'

'What?'

'It's in my coat. My coat that's in the van.'

'Oh, smooth, Major. Real smooth.'

Kim put the mirror back and wiped her fingerprints off before banging her hand on the sink in frustration.

'Something wrong?'

She spun around so fast, she was surprised she didn't snap her neck. Why did he keep sneaking up on her like that? How long had he been standing there? 'Harry!' Her heart rate pounded in fright. 'You scared me. What are you doing off the lounge?' She crossed to him and raised a hand to the bump on his head, which was now turning a nice shade of purple. 'You should still be lying down.' The best tactical defence she'd discovered when someone was questioning her was to distract them and question them back.

She led him back to the lounge and sat him down, then reached for the torch and checked his pupils once more. Next, she checked his blood pressure and when he opened his mouth to say something, she popped a thermometer in. Taking his pulse, she counted the beats and finally his obs were done. She packed the equipment away in his medical kit, gathered up the ice packs he'd discarded and took them into the kitchen.

'Permission to speak?' He'd followed her into the kitchen and once more she hadn't heard him.

'Do you own stealth shoes or something? Stop sneaking up on me.'

'You're very jumpy tonight.'

She forced a smile. 'I'm jumpy all the time.' Kim shrugged and turned the kettle on once more. 'I was just about to make the tea before but you were snoozing so peacefully it seemed a shame to wake you.'

'I'm sure.' He came and sat on a stool at his kitchen bench and watched as she made tea. 'Milk, no sugar,' he said.

'The opposite of how you take your coffee.'

'Good memory.' He paused, his gaze guarded. 'Thank you for taking care of me.'

'You're welcome.'

'You make an excellent nurse.'

She smiled. 'Let's hope I can impress you as much with my doctoring skills.'

'Have you done any nursing?'

'No. Being a doctor was all I really wanted to do.'

'I hope you don't take this the wrong way, but I find your age fascinating—I mean in that you're only doing your service year now.'

Kim merely shrugged and poured the water into the cups. 'Life happens.'

'Do you have siblings? Are your parents alive?'

'No and yes. How about you? Siblings?'

'I have two sisters. Lydia is a teacher. She and her husband have been working in Rwanda for the past few years.'

'Admirable.' She handed him his cup.

'My other sister, Zoe, is in Melbourne, doing her final year at medical school.'

'Quite a bit younger than you?'

He nodded. 'Both of them are. I think Zoe felt more comfortable doing her training in Melbourne, away from big brother's overprotectiveness.'

'And your parents?'

'Retired and enjoying the good life. Last I heard, they were going on a cruise on the QE-II.'

'Wow.' She sipped at her tea and sighed. 'I wish my parents would do something like that. All they do is stay in their nice, comfortable circle and worry about me.'

'Worrying about children is a parent's prerogative.'

'I know.'

'But it gets a bit much sometimes?'

'Yes.'

'Do they live close? Do you see them often?'

Kim hesitated. Telling people about her private life didn't come naturally. She was always suspicious and her top priority was to always protect her parents. If Harry was indeed on the inside of what she was investigating, she might be putting her parents in danger if she told him anything.

'They're not too far away and, yes, I see them as often as I can.'

'You're not very good at trusting,' he stated, still watching her closely.

'Who is?' She shrugged and took a big gulp of her tea. She breathed in at the same time and started choking. As a ploy it worked, and Harry quickly stood and patted her on the back.

She smiled weakly up at him and nodded when he asked if she was all right.

'Nice save,' Tammy said in her ear.

Tammy's voice in her ear was a timely reminder that she should be getting out of there.

Kim tipped the rest of her tea down the sink and rinsed the cup. 'Probably safer if I don't drink the rest of that,' she said, and turned to face him. She'd thought he'd sat down again but he hadn't. He was standing quite close and she instantly felt that enormous tug of attraction which existed between them.

She gazed up into his eyes and knew she couldn't have moved, even if she'd wanted to. 'Harry,' she tried, and cleared her throat, desperately trying to find strength to say what she needed to say. 'Harry, about before, I—'

'No. Don't say anything.' He placed two fingers on her lips and Kim gasped at the contact. She swallowed and tried to shift back but only came up against the bench. 'I've had a few bad experiences dating staff at the hospital and vowed to myself I wouldn't do it again, but with you, Kimberlie, I don't think I can keep that vow. I want to see you again.'

'You will. At the hospital.'

'You know what I mean.' He edged closer.

Kim buried her face in her hands and shook her head. 'Don't, Harry.' She dropped her hands and looked up at him, her gaze imploring. 'Don't do this, Harry.'

'What? Don't do what?' He gripped her shoulders. 'Tell me, Kimberlie. What is it?'

'I can't get involved with you. I just can't.'

'Why? Is there someone else?'

'No.' The word escaped her lips before she could turn it into a lie. Grasping at straws, she said, 'I need to concentrate on my job.' That much at least was true. 'I've worked too hard to get where I am and I still have a long way to go. Getting into a relationship or even just casual dating has to be put off at least for the next four to five years until I qualify. Surely you must realise that.'

He nodded but didn't let her go, didn't take his hands off her shoulders, and their warmth continued to spread through her.

'Can we still look into Mr Japarlin's death together?'

She sucked in a breath and nodded. 'Yes, but I'm not even sure I should be taking time away from study for that.'

'If it becomes too involved you can drop it, but for now it's definitely a good excuse for us to spend time together. Platonically,' he added, and stepped even closer. 'Well, almost.' He bent his head and brushed his lips over hers. Kim felt herself capitulating and within the next instant her arms were around his neck and she was kissing him back with ardent fervour.

This time the kiss was not sweet, sedate or even mildly soft. It was powerful, passionate and even a little punishing. Kim met his hunger and was more than pleased when he pressed his body against hers. The fire that ripped through her was immediate and one moment after the next, new explosions erupted.

He pulled back, gasping for air as he bent to trace hot, fiery kisses along her neck and up towards her ear.

Her ear. Her *right* ear. Which contained her earpiece!

Kim grabbed a handful of hair and jerked his head backwards before he had a chance to see it. He winced in pain and she belatedly remembered the bruise on the back of his neck.

'Ooh, sorry. Sorry, Harry.' She twisted out of his grasp and he didn't try to stop her. 'I'm sorry.' She shook her head and was surprised to find tears beginning to well in her eyes. 'I'm sorry, Harry. I just…I just can't.'

She swiped at a tear and shook her head before turning and fleeing his apartment.

Harry didn't follow her. He just watched her go. He raised a hand to his head and felt the spot where she'd just grabbed his hair and jerked his head backwards. It hadn't been hard—not as hard as his attacker. Interesting, though, that his attacker and Kimberlie had used the same manoeuvre.

Now that he thought more about it, when he'd slammed his attacker into the wall, the body structure had been different from a man's. He'd had his fair share of rough and tumbles during his rugby days at university so he knew what it was like to tackle a man. No, his attacker had been decidedly feminine…and then Kimberlie had shown up.

He walked into the lounge room where she'd left the bag she'd brought. He reached in and pulled out a new shirt, which he stared at for a moment before putting it back in the bag and crossing to his apartment alarm. As he went through the steps to insert a new code, he pondered the things he knew about Kimberlie.

She was older than the usual service registrar but didn't want to say why.

She was a natural in Theatre and he wondered whether she had more qualifications than she was letting on.

She hadn't trusted him enough to tell him even the basics about her family.

She had thumped his bathroom sink, but that could have been because she'd been angry with herself for kissing him.

Kissing... Harry breathed in deeply as he made his way to the bathroom. He stood in the middle of the room and remembered how incredible it had been to have his mouth on hers. It was everything he'd imagined and more—much more.

Harry opened the mirror which hid his safe. Had she found the safe? Had it made her think *he* was hiding something? He quickly entered the code and checked the contents. Everything was still there. His business papers, his will and his list...the list of suspects in Japarlin's death. He glanced down the list and stopped when he came to Kimberlie's name.

Was she involved somehow? Was she deceiving him with her charm and natural beauty? Was he playing right into her hands? He despised being lied to but if she was trying to cover up something, he wanted to be the one to uncover her secrets. Besides, so long as he kept control of the situation, there was no way he could get hurt.

Again, he seemed to have more questions than answers, and his gut reaction told him that the answers lay with Kimberlie Mason.

CHAPTER FIVE

WHETHER Harry was in the hospital on Sunday or not, Kim had no idea. It was a busy day and she managed to finally catch a lunch-break around three o'clock. Jerry came over and sat with her.

'Hectic day, huh?' Jerry sipped his coffee.

'You can say that again.'

'You did well in Theatre just now.'

'Thanks.'

'You should have no problem getting onto the training programme at the end of this year. I've heard that Harry's equally impressed with your skills and if you have him recommending you, there'll be no question of you not being accepted.'

Kim shrugged and smiled, taking another bite of her salad roll. 'I guess I'll find out at the end of the year,' she remarked, trying to be noncommittal. 'How about you? Did you have to wait long to move from being a lowly service registrar to being on the programme?'

'No. I was one of the lucky ones.'

'Ha. From the gossip I've heard, you're touted as the next brilliant general surgeon to come out of Sydney General.'

Jerry smiled. It wasn't a smile of conceit but rather one of unabashed pride. Kim decided she liked him. 'I've had good role models and a clear direction. My sister and her husband are orthopaedic surgeons over at the New South Wales Children's Hospital, my dad was a doctor and since I was about fifteen I knew I wanted to become a surgeon.'

Kim nodded. Of course, she knew all about Jerry Mayberry's background from the file she had on him. His parents had died when he'd been quite young and he and his younger brother had been left in the guardianship of his adopted older sister.

'It's rare, nowadays, to hear of someone so young having such a large goal in front of them. Most teenagers don't have a clue what they want to do, and rightly so. How are you supposed to know what you want to do when you're just starting to figure out what life's all about?'

Jerry nodded. 'How about you?'

She shrugged. 'Knew all along I wanted to do medicine.'

'Then how come you're quite a bit older than the usual service registrar?'

She'd fallen into that one and decided to use humour to get her way out of it. 'I'm not that old. I'm only thirty-two. How old are you?'

'Thirty-one.'

'There you go, then. Anyway, I guess you could say I took a few detours here and there.' Well, that was kind of true. Her involvement with ASIS certainly hadn't been planned. Surely that could be considered a kind of detour?

'But you've got there in the end. Good for you.'

'Thanks.' Kim shoved the last bite of her roll into her mouth and at that instant her pager beeped. Jerry's beeped at the same time. They both smiled.

'Time to get back to work, Dr Mason,' he said.

A few hours later, Tammy picked Kim up from the hospital and drove her back to her apartment. 'What about Jerry Mayberry?' Tammy asked as they went through the files once more.

Kim shook her head. 'Seems clean to me. He has no connection with Tarparnii, has never been to the country and was standing beside me the whole time we were in Theatre. Besides, I've met his brother-in-law, James Crosby, a few times. Even had dinner with James and his wife Holly a few years back. They're nice, honest people.'

Kim shook her head again. 'If Jerry Mayberry's involved in this, I'm a monkey's uncle.'

'You're that sure about him.'

'Yes, but I'll still keep a close eye on him.'

'Not too close or Harry will get jealous.'

'Oh, stop.' Kim threw a cushion at her friend.

'Do you think it might cause trouble if Jerry mentions your name to his sister or brother-in-law? Will that blow your cover?'

Kim frowned. 'I hadn't thought of that. Hmm. They're quite a close-knit family. It might but if it does we can deal with it then.'

'You think he'll keep quiet?'

'Yes, I do.'

'OK. What about the theatre nurse, Ni Kartu?'

'I was hoping to catch up with Ni some time tomorrow. I have a clinic in the morning so hopefully after that I can persuade him to join me for a coffee. He's reputed to be somewhat of a ladies' man so if I ask him out, he's bound to accept.'

'Take him off site. A coffee-shop would be better. Let me know the time and place and I'll be there.'

'Good.'

'Next…' Tammy sorted through the files. 'John McPhee, anaesthetist.'

'He's a tough one to get close to. Being a service registrar, I don't have many dealings with top-of-the-line anaesthetists. With his lackeys, yes, but he's head of Anaesthetics and way out of my league as a junior doctor. We'll have to think of something.'

'OK. Perhaps you should have gone with Harry to the heads-of-unit dinner last night.'

'Perhaps, but it was better to get a good look around his apartment.'

'You still need to get into that safe.'

'I know. I thought of calling around again to see how he was recovering from the, uh…' She paused.

'The whipping you gave him yesterday evening?'

'I didn't mean to.' Kim closed her eyes and hung her head. 'I feel so guilty.'

'Get rid of the guilt. It's happened and won't help further your investigation. For all we know, Harry Buchanan *is* the enemy and then you'll feel better for knocking him out.'

'Yeah, but I won't feel better about kissing him.'

Tammy grinned. 'You still haven't told me all the details.'

'And I'm not going to.'

'Hey, last night you said you'd clue me in.'

'That was to stop you yacking on in my ear!'

Tammy threw a cushion at Kim. 'I was very restrained. I could have talked all the time you were playing kissy-face with the sexy doctor.'

Kim giggled. 'Kissy-face?'

Tammy made some exaggerated slurping noises and Kim laughed again. 'Cut it out. You're embarrassing me.' The phone rang and she snatched it up, ignoring her friend. 'Dr Mason.'

'Kimberlie.'

All he had to do was say her name and she was a mass of tingles. 'Harry!' Tammy's slurping noises increased and Kim threw two cushions back at her.

He paused. 'Am I interrupting you?'

'No.' Kim stood up and started pacing the room. 'Tammy's here and she's making a general nuisance of herself.'

'Hi, Harry,' Tammy called, grinning wildly at her friend.

'Er…hello,' he said a little hesitantly.

'He says to leave me alone and stop picking on me,' Kim related. Tammy snorted.

'I didn't say that at all,' he protested, but Kim only laughed.

'What can I do for you, Harry? Render more first aid? Attend a heads-of-department function?

Or just generally discuss the incredibly busy day I've had?'

'Well, it's funny you should ask,' he began, and she felt her smile increase. 'I was wondering if you're free for coffee? Just for half an hour. I won't keep you long.'

Kim glanced at the clock. It was only half past eight so coffee would be fine, especially if it was in a public place. Although she needed to get back into his apartment to check out his safe, she didn't think she should suggest coming around to his place now. No, that would be far too dangerous. She was still trying to recover from what had happened last night.

'Or are you about to start studying?' he added when she didn't reply straight away.

'With Tammy here? I've got Buckley's and no hope.'

'I take it that means no?'

'No to studying and yes to coffee. Just half an hour, though,' she said. 'Is it anything…exciting you wish to discuss?'

'I'd rather not say on the phone.' His tone had changed from teasingly sexy to one of wariness. Whatever he had to tell her *had* to be about Japarlin, or something connected with it.

'Where do you want to meet?'

'There's a café two blocks from the hospital. We can meet there or, as it's late, I can pick you up and then we can go.'

'That's OK. I'll meet you there. Tammy can drop me on her way home.'

'Excellent. Fifteen minutes?'

'Sounds like a plan. See you then.' Kim disconnected the call and told Tammy of her plans.

'I'll get the agency to send a surveillance van.'

'There isn't time. I'll take a tape recorder. It'll be fine.'

'You're sure?'

'Yes.'

'OK, then. It's your call but I'll hang around in the car just in case you need back-up.'

'It's coffee, Tam.'

'You honestly believe the sexy doctor only has coffee on his mind?' She wiggled her eyebrows suggestively.

Kim laughed. 'No. Maybe coffee and a bit of espionage talk but as far as he and I are concerned, I made it clear to him last night that I can't get involved.' She headed for her bedroom and flung open her wardrobe. 'We're just going to be friends. Friends and colleagues who are looking into a suspicious death.' She flicked her hand along some clothes. 'Oh, man! I have *nothing* to wear!'

* * *

Harry stood as Kim walked across to the table where he sat. He quickly held out her chair. 'You look beautiful.' His words were soft and intimate, his breath brushing over her exposed nape and causing goose-bumps to ripple over her arm.

'Thank you.'

He returned to his seat and eyed her speculatively. 'It *is* all right for one platonic friend to compliment another?'

Kim smiled. 'Yes, Harry. Compliment away.' The way he was looking at her was anything but platonic, but she ignored that for the moment. She was also glad she didn't have Tammy or anyone else listening to her conversation. If he said anything of great consequence, it would be picked up by the tape in her handbag and she would be the person to transcribe the notes, therefore leaving out any irrelevant stuff…stuff like personal compliments.

She'd chosen brown trousers and a russet halter-neck top. She'd clipped half of her unruly curls back from her face and the only jewellery she wore was a pair of gold earrings her parents had given her. Her outfit was casual yet pretty and as she'd had a whole ten minutes to change after Harry's phone call, she was pleased at the compliment he'd given her.

'I like your earrings.'

She fingered the small diamond drops at her lobes. 'A gift from my parents.'

'That's nice. My mother never gives me presents I can wear in public.'

Kim raised her eyebrows in surprise. 'Surely you're not going to leave me hanging there?'

The waiter came and took their order and Kim prodded him again. 'Come on, Harry. Give.'

'She gives me underwear. Every birthday, without fail since as far back as I can remember. She says it's a mother's prerogative.'

Kim remembered the loud and outlandish boxer shorts she'd found in his drawer and her smile increased. 'Nice sedate ones, I hope.'

'Far from it. Cartoon characters, silly joke ones.'

Kim put her elbows on the table and leaned forward. 'What's on the ones you're wearing now?'

Harry grimaced. 'Who brought this subject up?' he asked rhetorically.

'You did,' she answered. 'Come on.'

'Smiley faces.'

'Smiley faces,' Kim repeated, and chuckled. 'Interesting. Who would have thought the head of General Surgery, the brilliant Harry Buchanan, walks around the hospital with wild and outlandish underwear beneath his conservative suits?'

'Not many people, I'll bet, and if my underwear suddenly becomes the topic of the gossip mill, I'll know where it started.'

'With Elaine?' Kim settled back in her chair, her smile slowly disappearing.

He watched her for a moment. 'Jealous?'

'If we weren't in a platonic relationship, perhaps, but as we are…no. Although I have to say, Harry, that Elaine Parkinson doesn't strike me as your type.'

'She's not.'

'Good.'

The waiter brought their coffees and once more Kim leaned forward. Beneath the table, she slipped her hand into her bag and switched on the tape recorder. 'Now,' she said quietly, 'what did you want to discuss?'

Harry sipped his coffee and added another sugar. 'The officials from Tarparnii arrived a few hours ago.'

Kim nodded even though this was information she already knew.

'I know one of the officials,' he said, not looking at her but concentrating on stirring the sugar into his coffee. 'He told me they'd received information that if Japarlin underwent surgery on Australian soil, an attempt would be made on his life.'

Kim's eyes widened. 'They have evidence of this?'

'He didn't say.'

'So it *was* murder.'

'The Tarparniian government are treating it as suspicious. The autopsy is being performed tomorrow morning and they won't be publicly releasing the findings until the Tarparniians are satisfied.'

'If they discover anything…untoward, do you think they'll announce it as murder or stick with the original story of the myocardial infarction?'

'I don't know.'

'What about our government? Doesn't Australia have some government officials assisting the Tarparniians?' She knew perfectly well that this was the case but wanted to know how strong Harry's contact was.

'Yes, but the Tarparniians want their own doctor to perform the autopsy—that's who my friend is. He's the forensic pathologist they've brought with them.'

'Is he honest?'

'Yes. He's a good man. We've worked together many times when I've held my clinics in Tarparnii. He'll help by doing general pathology work free.'

'At least there's someone you can trust doing the work.'

'Yes, but now I'm concerned for him. What if he finds something that indicates the minister was murdered? What type of strain is that going to put on our two countries?'

'Do you think either government will try to keep it quiet?'

'I don't know. My friend did say he thinks some of the officials who brought him here wanted Japarlin dead.'

Kim sat back in her chair. 'Oh, my.'

'Exactly.'

'Well, what can *we* do?'

'We can keep an eye on my friend.'

'How? Neither of us are forensic pathologists. We won't be allowed anywhere near the morgue.'

'As I was the surgeon in charge of the operation, my friend is going to ask that I'm present at the autopsy.'

'So you won't be in clinic tomorrow?'

'No. I'm sure you, Jerry and Dr Edington will do fine.'

'Don't worry about it. Will you page me when you're done?' Kim reached out and took his hand in hers. 'Please?'

Harry saw genuine concern in her gaze and it both surprised and warmed him. It had been a long time since he'd met someone like Kimberlie. One minute she seemed so genuinely concerned for him and the next…she left him with more questions about her behaviour.

The gravitational pull he felt towards her grew each time he saw her and although he'd resisted it in the beginning, he now came to accept it as fact. Kimberlie Mason was someone he definitely wanted to know better and the fact that she seemed to reciprocate that was of great importance to him. Of course, her excuse last night as to why she couldn't date him was quite valid, and he wanted to show her he respected her need to put her medical career before any personal relationship, but right now, when she looked at him with those soulful green eyes, he found it almost impossible to follow through in that respect. He wanted to hold her, touch her, kiss her. Now that he knew how perfect she felt in his arms, the warmth of her body, the experience of her lips melding with his, he only wanted it more.

Instead, he dragged in a breath and slowly exhaled before giving her hand a small squeeze and pulling away. 'I'll do my best to page you when we're done.'

'Thank you. I'd appreciate it. I guess they'll put a rush on the path results. Will you be privy to those, too?'

'At this stage, I'm not sure. I think the Tarparniians are going to want to see them first.'

'They'll have to duke it out with our government…I expect,' she added quickly. She drained her coffee and glanced at her watch. 'Listen, Harry. As much as I'd love to sit here and chat, I—'

'I know, you have studying to do.' He motioned the waiter over and paid for their drinks before standing. 'Let me drive you home.'

Kim nodded and as they walked, she flicked off her tape recorder. They'd just arrived at his car when her phone rang. 'Dr Mason,' she said quickly, hoping it wasn't her boss from the agency.

'All done?' Tammy asked.

'Hi, Tam,' she said, more for Harry's benefit than anything else.

'Get everything you need?'

'Yes. I'm going home to study. You know, you're worse than my mother.'

Tammy chuckled. 'OK. Call me when you get in.'

'OK. Bye.' She disconnected the call. 'I like your car, Harry. I meant to tell you the other day.' He drove a dark green Jaguar and she slid comfortably into the leather seats. 'How long have you had her?' she asked as he sat in the driver's seat and pulled on his seat belt. She followed suit.

'Since I became a consultant. It was my gift to myself.'

'Hey, good idea. Think I'll set myself a similar goal, but not with a car.'

'You don't drive?'

'I do but I prefer not to.'

'Why?'

'I turn into a madman—or should that be madwoman?—when I get behind the wheel, especially of some snazzy little sports car like this. Take me out on a race track and I'm fine.'

'Sounds scary.'

Kim merely shrugged. 'I know my limitations.'

It was only a short drive to her apartment and once he'd cut the engine, he came around to open the door for her. Kim, who wasn't used to being on the receiving end of such gentlemanly treatment, was already half out of the car by the time he came around.

'Oh! Thank you.' She stepped onto the footpath and smiled at him. Slowly, the smile began to slip from her face as their gazes locked. The atmosphere around them intensified, as though there was a little bubble containing only the two of them. The noise of the city streets, the car fumes, the streetlight casting a glow down on them—everything faded into nothingness as they simply stood there and stared at each other.

Kim sucked a breath into her lungs and forced her legs to move backwards. She swallowed over the dryness in her throat. 'Thanks…for the coffee.'

Harry cleared his throat. 'My pleasure.'

The deep huskiness of his voice couldn't disguise the pent-up passion. It was almost her undoing and she clenched her free hand at her side, the other holding her bag so firmly she thought she'd crush the tape recorder to smithereens.

Again she took a deep breath. 'Don't forget to page me or call me or whatever the instant you're finished tomorrow.'

'I won't.' He closed the passenger door and shifted away. 'I'll wait until you get inside.'

Oh, he was *so* sweet. She smiled. 'See you tomorrow.'

'Don't study for too long. The last thing I'll need tomorrow is a grumpy service registrar.'

Kim smiled as she started to walk away, glad they'd fought their way through that intense moment. 'I'll do my best.' She headed for the door to her apartment block and stopped and turned. 'Goodnight, Harry.'

'Sleep sweet, Kimberlie.'

'Is everything set?' Kim asked Tammy the following morning. She was sitting in the cubbyhole of an office afforded to service registrars. Her desk was covered in casenotes for her attention and she was due on the ward in two minutes. She cradled the phone between her ear and shoulder while she quickly wrote up some notes and signed off on them.

'Everything's in place. Ivan's installed a small camera in the room where they'll be doing the autopsy so we'll be able to see and hear everything.'

'Good. We'll rendezvous for debrief tonight? Dinner at my apartment?'

'Sure. Chinese?'

'Yum. OK. Page me if you need anything else.'

'Will do. Bye.'

Kim hurriedly wrote up another set of casenotes before shrugging into her white coat for the ward round. She gathered up the notes she'd completed and dropped them off at the stenographer's office on her way to the ward.

Harry was there in his crisp navy suit and she immediately wondered what kind of boxer shorts he was wearing today. Her hungry gaze quickly scanned him before she moved further into the room. He looked so neat and tidy—with the way he discarded clothes sloppily around his apartment, he was obviously a regular patron at the dry cleaners. Kim smiled at the thought and sat down.

'Having a good morning, Kim?' Jerry Mayberry asked.

Kim checked her watch. 'Sure. When you consider I've been awake for a whole hour and a half, it hasn't been too bad.'

Jerry chuckled.

'*If* everyone's finished their morning socialising,' Harry growled, glaring directly at Kim and Jerry, 'we'll start the ward round.' Harry turned to the first set of casenotes and began explaining about the patient.

'I guess Harry's been up for more than an hour and a half,' Jerry whispered, and Kim had to choke back her laughter.

Harry stopped speaking and glared at her before slowly continuing. What was his problem? Was he nervous about the autopsy? Concerned they'd find something that indicated Harry had been at fault? Were the Tarparniian officials here to pin this murder on Harry? She shook her head, glad a camera had been installed so ASIS would be able to monitor everything that went on.

'You don't agree, Dr Mason?' Harry asked sceptically.

Kim met his smouldering gaze. He really was in a bad mood. She also realised she'd been frowning at him and shaking her head so obviously he'd thought she'd been commenting on what he'd been saying about poor old Mr Dracouski. She quickly recalled the case and cleared her throat.

She was more than willing to give her opinion about the case, and *in* her opinion the decision to operate had come a little late, which was why Mr Dracouski was now having these post-operative problems. She opened her mouth to speak but caught herself in time, remembering she was there as a service registrar.

Instead, she sucked in a breath, knowing Harry was about to bawl her out. 'I'm sorry, Dr Buchanan. My mind had wandered elsewhere and I wasn't listening. I apologise. Please, continue.'

She watched Harry's jaw clench and a vein in his forehead looked as though it was going to burst. He hadn't looked this stressed since right after Mr Japarlin had died on the operating table.

He stared at her for a moment and she waited, the whole room waited for him to speak. Finally, he looked away and repeated what he'd just said. Kim frowned. Why hadn't he yelled at her? She'd clearly been at fault and had openly admitted it.

'I think our Dr Buchanan fancies you,' Jerry whispered as they all filed out of the room to go and greet their patients. 'And he's just made it clear to every person in that room.'

'Why? Because he didn't wipe the floor with me?'

'Exactly.'

'But I thought he preferred honesty from his staff? If they make a mistake, he wants the truth, not excuses.'

'Even so, he still would have told you off—probably not as harshly—but he didn't.' Jerry raised his eyebrows suggestively before heading to the front of the ward round and starting to give an update on the first patient's condition. It wasn't until they'd been around to all the patients that Harry said, 'Dr Mason, please see me in my office before clinic.' Then stormed off.

'You were saying?' she said to Jerry.

He shrugged. 'Perhaps I was wrong…but I'm usually not.'

Kim headed up to general surgery administration where Harry's office was situated and knocked twice on his door.

'Come in.'

She walked in and shut the door behind her. He was pacing his room, completely out of sorts, and she was instantly concerned.

'Harry? What is it?' He didn't answer. 'Is it the autopsy? What about your friend? Is he all right?'

'It's *you*.'

'Pardon?'

He stopped pacing and raked a hand through his hair, making it stand on end. 'I can't sleep, I can't think properly. Kimberlie, you're driving me insane and all you can do is laugh and flirt with other staff members and then politely apologise for not listening to me when I speak!'

'You should have told me off publicly.'

'Are you interested in Jerry Mayberry?'

'Pardon?'

'You heard. Answer the question.'

'No.'

'Are you interested in me?'

'Harry!'

'Kimberlie. I need an answer.'

'Why?'

'I told you why. I hardly slept last night and last night was the one night I *really* needed to sleep. A lot is happening today and I need to be alert. Instead, I'm more concerned about whether you're really attracted to me or not. I apologise if I'm putting you on the spot but I need to know.'

Kim shook her head. 'Harry,' she said softly, and he closed his eyes. She needed to push him away, to tell him there could never be anything between them. She was there to do a job he knew nothing about. She was lying to him and she knew that the one thing Harry Buchanan couldn't stand was people lying to him. Her job took her all over the world and Harry's life was here in Sydney. There was no way she could admit the attraction she felt for him. It wasn't fair, to her or to him.

This was the moment. This was the time, yet...she couldn't do it.

He opened his eyes. 'Kimberlie?' He stood with his hands clenched into fists at his sides, his jaw clamped tightly as he waited.

'Am I interested in you?' She repeated his question, her tone tender and honest. 'Of course I am, Harry, but I can't—' Whatever she'd been about to say was cut short as he covered the remaining distance between them and gathered her into his arms, pressing his mouth to hers.

The kiss was possessive, punishing and… perfect. Her body sighed against his as she clung limply to the lapels of his suit jacket. His mouth moved over hers in such a masterful way it was all she could do not to slither down his body and end up a pool of mush at his feet.

He was making her swoon. She'd heard the word before, read about it in romance novels, seen it at the movies, but she'd never felt it before and he was definitely making her swoon. Her head was light, her body was lifeless and all she wanted was for his lips to keep on delivering their sweet pleasure over and over again until the end of time.

The intercom on his desk buzzed to life and although Kim jumped, Harry didn't let her go. Instead, he finished kissing her at his leisure before guiding her over to a chair where, with a satisfied smile, he helped her to sit.

'Yes?' He answered his secretary.

'They're ready at the morgue.'

'Thank you.' He turned to face Kim, his smile still in place. 'I have to go.'

'Yeah.'

'Kimberlie?' He chuckled when she didn't move. 'Are you going to be all right for clinic?'

'Don't be so smug, Harry. It ruins your pretty face.'

He snorted with derision. 'Men don't have *pretty* faces, Kimberlie.' He held out a hand to help her up but she brushed it away, forcing her mind to work and her body to follow its signals.

'Whatever.' She sucked in a deep breath and stood. 'You be careful down there,' she warned.

All humour disappeared from his face and he nodded. 'I will.'

'Page me when it's over?'

'Yes.'

Kim's pager beeped and she switched it off, glancing at the clock. The autopsy should be over by now and she was eager to find out what had happened. Instead, she returned her attention to her patient.

'Everything seems to be healing nicely, Karin.'

'I can't believe I don't have a huge scar. My friend had her appendix out and she has a huge scar.'

'Done via a laparotomy, she would have. You had yours removed via laparoscopy which is why there are just a few little scars.'

'I'm really happy.'

'I'm glad.'

'Do I need to come back again?'

'Only if you have problems. Other than that, you're free to go.' And so am I, she added silently as she wrote up Karin's notes and took them out to the outpatients stenographer.

She checked the number on her pager and was surprised to see it wasn't Harry's number but Tammy's. She headed downstairs to the basement where she'd found an out-of-the-way public phone and quickly called her friend.

'We have a problem.'

'What? Is Harry all right?'

'He's more than all right. He stole a sample of the patient's liver.'

CHAPTER SIX

'I NEED you to find out why he took it, Kim. I have no idea why he did but the camera picked it up as clear as day. His friend who performed the autopsy palmed it to him. No one else saw and, believe me, I've double- and triple-checked the recording. He's quite a guy, your Harry.'

'He'll want tests done on it straight away.' Kim thought for a moment. 'Might be worthwhile checking around the path labs. There are quite a few, but if we can find the one he's sent it to, we could get a copy of the results.'

'He wouldn't use the hospital path department, would he? I mean, if he has a friend or a contact there.'

'I can look into that.'

'No. I'll get Ivan to do it. I still want you to get a look inside his safe. So, what do you think he wanted the sample for?'

'Perhaps he thinks this will answer some of the questions he has.'

'Why would you take the sample? What tests would you get done?'

Kim thought for a moment. 'Top of the list would be to find out if any unordered substance had been put into the drip. It would show up in the liver.'

'Or he could be trying to cover his tracks.'

Kim closed her eyes and shook her head. 'No. Harry's not involved in the death, he's just trying to figure it out.'

'That's what your instincts tell you?'

'Yes.'

'That's not your hormones talking?'

'No!'

'Hey, just checking. For the record, I agree with you. Moss is happy with what you've turned up so far and that Harry seems to be clean. We just need to get a look in his safe to be one hundred per cent sure.'

'I'll do it tonight.' Her words were a little impatient. 'I'm sorry. I just know he's not involved.'

'Moss wants it by the book.'

Something in Tammy's tone struck a chord with Kim. 'Why is Moss so interested in Harry?'

'Let's just say that Moss is highly impressed by him.'

'No.' Her voice was firm.

'What?'

'You told me Moss was highly impressed with *me* and the next think I knew I was working for ASIS. I don't want Harry dragged into this life.'

'I understand where you're coming from, Kim, I really do, but this isn't your call.'

'Well, if Moss is so impressed by him, why doesn't he just bring Harry in and ask him why he took the sample?' Kim was furious. Moss was up to his usual games, not caring that Harry had a life but only how Harry could be used by ASIS.

'Calm down. For the moment, I'll put a tail on Harry to see which path lab he goes to.'

Kim sighed heavily, knowing her friend was right. 'If we don't let him follow through with his initial plan, we might never know why he took it, although I'm sure it's because he knows he won't be privy to the official report. I'll talk to him. Chances are he'll tell me all about it.'

'OK. Moss wants a report by the end of the day.'

Kim was silent, her eyes closed as she tried to hold a pounding headache at bay.

'Kim?'

'Hmm?'

'Look on the bright side. If Moss is looking to recruit Harry—and I'm not saying for sure that he is—at least it shows Moss thinks Harry's innocent in Japarlin's death.'

'I guess. Is there any word back from the lab regarding the bins which were removed from the theatre last Friday? Surely they'd have the results back by now.'

'Moss has them. I have a meeting with him in an hour.'

Kim's pager beeped again. She checked it, hoping it would be Harry, hoping he was calling to tell her he'd taken the sample and why he'd done it. Instead, it was the number for Theatre.

'I have to go. I'm in Theatre this afternoon.'

'With Harry?'

'It's his list. Whether or not he makes it is another thing. Jerry usually takes control when Harry's not there, but hopefully he will be today.'

'If you get a chance—'

'I'll try and find out why he did it,' Kim finished. 'I'll speak to you later.' She headed up to Theatres for the elective operating list. 'What's on the slate for today?' she asked Jerry.

'As if you didn't know. You're the one who booked the patients.'

She smiled at him. 'Just trying to keep you on your toes.'

'So, did the boss bawl you out?'

Kim looked down at her feet, wondering how to answer. 'In a way.'

Jerry gasped. 'You like him, don't you,' he stated.

Kim glanced up and quickly looked around the corridor they were standing in. Jerry looked around, too. 'It's OK. I won't tell a soul. I loathe hospital gossip,' he said, an interested smile on his face, his eyes sparkling with repressed delight.

'Don't we all,' she muttered, as she walked off to the female changing rooms. The list was full but quite routine. Two cholecystectomies, one appendicectomy, one hernia removal and two vasectomies. They were just scrubbing for the hernia operation when Harry joined them at the scrub sink.

'How's it been going?' he asked Jerry.

'Good. Mr Fitzsymonds's appendix burst just after removal so I've started him on IV antibiotics, which should combat any infection he might suffer, but we're sure we got it all, aren't we, Kim?'

'It looked perfect to me,' she replied, watching Harry closely. Was he going to tell her about the liver sample? She felt like dragging him off into a corner, tying him to a chair, roping his hands together and sticking a great big light in his face, demanding he tell her the truth…and then kissing him senseless.

Her stomach churned and she closed her eyes for a moment, working hard to get control of her thoughts. Harry had come to mean a great deal to her in a very short time and the way he kissed her was…magic.

'Kimberlie?' Harry's concerned tone made her eyes snap open. 'Are you all right?'

She straightened her shoulders and forced a smile. 'I'm fine.' She returned her attention to her hands and finished scrubbing. She had to remind herself that *she* wasn't being entirely honest with Harry so she shouldn't judge him if he kept things from her. She did, however, need to keep a close eye on him. If only he didn't make her feel so…feminine, so cherished, so alive with just one simple caress of his gaze.

She glanced up at him again and found him watching her. Jerry had finished scrubbing so, for the moment, it was just the two of them at the sink. Kim cleared her throat. 'How'd the autopsy go?' she asked in a low voice.

Harry didn't reply immediately but held her gaze. 'Free for dinner?'

The smile that spread across her face was as real as the sunshine in the sky. 'Why, yes. I am.' This was good. This was very good. Harry was going to tell her what had happened at the autopsy and tell her he'd taken the sample. Yes!

Her previous black mood immediately lifted and it was all due to the man standing next to her.

'Are you two ready to go or are you going to stand there making googly eyes at each other all day?' Jerry's voice brought Kim back to reality with a thump. Harry glowered at his registrar but Jerry merely shrugged. 'It was either me break the moment or have the scrub sister come in and catch you.'

Kim watched as a look of stunned amazement crossed Harry's face before he glanced at her. She shrugged as well, as though accepting the inevitability of the situation. Harry shook his head in disbelief, unable to believe he'd been so obvious with his attention and feelings towards her.

'Are we gossip yet?' he asked. 'Not that I care, but it might make life a little difficult for you.'

'Jerry's just too smart for his own good,' she replied.

'If that's all it is, that's fine.'

'I'd also suggest not asking her out to dinner over the scrub sink,' Jerry remarked quietly to his boss as both Harry and Kim elbowed off the taps. 'Anyone could have walked in.'

'Noted.'

They finished gowning and headed into Theatre for the hernia operation. Kim hadn't done one of these operations for a long time, so it was interesting not only to watch Harry work but to assist as well. He spoke while he worked, taking her through the procedure step by step, answering her questions and making sure she understood everything. He did things with such fluidity she was itching to adapt some of his techniques for her own personal use.

Once that was done, there were only two more patients to get through, and Harry insisted that Kim perform the second vasectomy. Jerry assisted her while her boss watched, and although she knew what she was doing, she was very conscious of Harry's gaze on her the whole time.

Finally the list was complete and she discovered they'd run half an hour over their scheduled operating time. 'There'll be red tape to cover for that,' she said as they walked towards the changing rooms.

'Tell me about it,' Harry muttered. Jerry went ahead of him into the male changing rooms, tactfully leaving them alone for a few minutes. 'Pick you up at seven?'

She raised her eyebrows. 'An early dinner?'

'You have to study this evening, Dr Mason,' he pointed out, and she smiled.

'So good of you to remember, Dr Buchanan. OK. I'll see you then.' Neither of them moved.

They both stayed exactly where they were, standing in the corridor outside the changing rooms—females on the left, males on the right—staring into each other's eyes.

Kim wanted nothing more than to lean forward and press her lips warmly to Harry's. There was hardly any physical distance between them and from the look in his eyes he mirrored the feelings she was desperately trying to get under control. It was clear he wanted to kiss her as much as she wanted him to. They both knew now was neither the time nor the place, but would they be able to fight the desire raging within them?

Although there wasn't much distance between them physically, Kim acknowledged that mentally there were chasms between them. Once Harry found out about her deception and what she was really doing in his department, he wouldn't want to have a bar of her.

There was also the fact that the attraction she felt for him couldn't really go anywhere. When she was finished with this job, she'd be going back to her latest army posting, which was in Queensland—unless ASIS had another job for her to do, in which case she might be going anywhere in the world. She and Harry—they could never be.

Holding onto that thought, she slowly eased the tension out of her body and sighed. 'See you later,' she said softly, and called upon superhuman strength from somewhere to help her turn away from him and enter the changing rooms.

As though on autopilot, she wandered through to her locker, removed her clothes and headed for the showers, turning the taps on so the cold, cold water could cascade over her, dousing the hot fire Harry always lit deep within her.

It wasn't fair. Why, when she found a guy she really liked, who she bonded with so easily, did he have to be unavailable to her? It *so* wasn't fair. She finished showering, dressed and headed out of Theatres, telling herself not to hang around in the hope she might run into Harry but instead to finish her work, then get herself home, see if Tammy had any news to report and start getting ready for her date.

Kim headed to the ward and checked on her patients, and by the time she finally headed outside it was almost six o'clock. She switched her mobile phone on and found two messages from Tammy. She sat down on the bench beside the main doorway to the hospital and listened to her messages.

'Call me when you get this. The meeting with Moss was interesting and we have some new information.'

'Kimmy—how much longer are you going to be? I'll be at your place around sevenish. I'll bring the new info then. Bye.'

Kim grimaced as she realised she'd made double plans for dinner, although she knew Tammy wouldn't mind breaking them, especially as her date with Harry might explain why he'd taken the sample from the autopsy.

She sighed and started to call Tammy back when a deep voice beside her said, 'That's a heavy sigh for a little lady.' She turned and was surprised to find Ni Kartu, who had been one of the nurses in Theatre when Mr Japarlin had died. He was also someone she'd been wanting to question.

'Busy day?' he asked, as he sauntered over to her side and sat down. He was very good-looking, his dark eyes, hair and skin giving him an air of mystery which she'd heard a lot of the women in the hospital were attracted to.

'Aren't they all?' She smiled and put her phone away. 'How's your day been?'

'About the same.'

'You know, I could really use a cup of coffee.'

His eyebrows rose at her forwardness. 'So could I. How about we go and find a coffee-shop…together?' He said the last word with emphasis and Kim had to stop herself from laughing out loud. She'd heard Ni Kartu was a bit of a ladies' man and knew she'd have no trouble getting his attention, but now it appeared she was going to have more trouble *losing* that attention.

'Let's go, then.' She was conscious of the time and knew she needed to get Ni to open up quite quickly if she was going to make it home in time to have a debrief with Tammy and get ready for her date.

Harry stopped beside his car, fished his keys out of his pocket and happened to look up in time to see Kimberlie heading out of the hospital grounds with Ni Kartu. He clenched his teeth, telling himself they were merely walking the same way together and that when they got to the traffic lights, Kimberlie would go one way and Ni would go the other. He waited.

No. They both went the same way. His hand tightened around the handle of his briefcase and he once more told himself it was nothing. Kimberlie had said earlier that she was interested in him and although the kisses they'd shared had literally rocked him off his axis, it didn't mean he had exclusivity on her time and who she spent it with.

Perhaps she was just getting to know a few more people at the hospital. That was good, wasn't it? Her contract was only for a three-month rotation and after that she was due to leave Sydney General to complete the rest of her service year in Queensland. So, yes, it was good that she was making friends here. Perhaps that would convince her to put in for a transfer and finish her training here…with him.

Kimberlie was so different from the women he had dated in the past. The way she kept putting her studying before him was driving him to distraction, even though he completely agreed with her. She was tight-lipped about herself, her family and her past. He'd noticed a few times she'd wanted to say something but had clammed up at the last minute. Something had obviously happened in her past to stop her from trusting people, and that was all right—but not when it came to her not trusting him!

He watched her walk with Ni until they were out of sight. Regardless of where she was going with the handsome theatre nurse, she had a date with him in an hour and there was no way he was letting her get out of it. Apart from the fact he wanted to see her, to kiss her, he wanted to tell her about the autopsy and what his friend had said.

Harry had had his own agenda for wanting to attend the autopsy, and the main item had been to get the sample from the patient. Thankfully, his friend agreed with him that something wasn't right and had willingly taken an extra sample just for him.

Both the Tarparnii government officials who had come to make sure everything went as planned for the autopsy had fainted when the stench of slightly decomposed human body had hit them. After the autopsy had been completed, his friend had secretly passed him the sample, which Harry had taken to a different pathology office from the one the hospital used and asked for a rush on the results. He needed the sample to see if there had been any unordered substances injected into the patient. If anything *had* been injected into the patient, it would show up in the liver first. Even though several pathology requests had gone out, Harry knew he wouldn't be privy to them for weeks to come.

Thankfully, the autopsy had proved once and for all that Harry hadn't done anything wrong, and for all intents and purposes Mr Japarlin *had* died of natural causes. He shook his head. There was still something very wrong going on and he was determined to discover what. It was gut instinct and he'd learned in the past to always follow his instincts.

'Harry.'

He turned at the sound of his name and saw John McPhee striding towards him. Harry jangled his car keys from his finger and smiled at his colleague.

'Managed to get out of Theatre on time?' Harry asked the anaesthetist.

'Thankfully. Listen, I'm glad I caught you. My wife and I are having a party on Friday night and we'd like you to attend. Nothing formal, but lots of drink, lots of food and lots of people. Bring a friend if you like.'

'Thanks.' Harry immediately thought about taking Kimberlie. Surely she could take one night off from studying.

'Anyway,' John continued, 'I have to meet my wife in a few minutes. I've left her alone at the shopping mall so if I don't stop her soon, I'm afraid my credit card will have been flexed way too much.' He chuckled. 'At least you single guys don't need to worry about things like that.'

'No, we have other things to worry about, like how to find the right woman.'

'The hospital grapevine says you haven't dated anyone since you broke up with Elaine.'

'I'm just picky. I made a mistake with Elaine and I don't intend to repeat it.'

John came a little closer. 'Actually, I saw you the other night in a coffee-shop with your new service registrar. She's a pretty thing.'

'Yes, she is,' Harry agreed, glancing in the direction Kimberlie had gone. Then he frowned and looked at his colleague. 'That was rather late in the evening, though. I'd have thought as you're now head of department, you could roster yourself off those awful late shifts.'

Was it his imagination or was John's smile slightly forced?

'No, I wasn't in Theatre that night. Just had a lot of paperwork to catch up on. With Mr Japarlin's death, there have been all sorts of extra "i"s to be dotted and "t"s to be crossed. The old paper trail never seems to disappear, regardless of how much the computer age has taken over. Anyway, it was just paperwork that night. You know.' John shrugged. 'The usual story.'

Harry nodded slowly and held up his own briefcase. 'I'm just about to start my catch-up for the evening.'

John's forced smile stayed in place. 'Hey, have you heard anything about the autopsy?'

'Yes. I was there. All went according to plan.'

'You were there? Why wasn't I asked?'

'As the surgeon in charge, they asked me merely as a courtesy.'

'Well, I'm a bit put out. As the anaesthetist in charge, why wasn't I offered the same courtesy?'

'I'm not sure. Perhaps you should check with Elaine in the morning.'

'Oh, never mind.' John seemed agitated. 'Do you know when the path results will be back?'

Harry shrugged. 'Few days. Tomorrow if they're lucky. As this was a top-priority case, they're bound to put a rush on it.' Harry watched John closely. 'Is there anything wrong?'

John immediately cleared his frown and smiled. 'No. No. Just the whole thing with the Tarparniians gives me the creeps. I don't know how you can go to that country and do clinics there.'

'People all around the world need good medical attention, John, and Tarparnii isn't the only country I visit.'

'No. Quite. Well, I'd better not keep you any longer. I'd better go save my credit card while I still have the chance.' He chuckled and headed off with a brief wave. Harry unlocked his car and climbed in, his mind running over the strange conversation. He hadn't received extra paperwork regarding the Foreign Minister's death. Why had John? Perhaps there were forms he was supposed to fill in but they'd been lost in bureaucratic red tape. He'd get his secretary to find out in the morning, otherwise he'd have Elaine on his case and that was the last thing he wanted right now.

Harry drove over the Sydney Harbour Bridge, his mind filled with thoughts about John and the strange conversation, as well as Kimberlie and where she'd been going with Ni Kartu. Why was it every day when he got up and went to work, he came home with far more questions which never seemed to find answers?

Ni Kartu continued to make amusing small talk as they waited for their coffees to arrive and Kim couldn't help enjoying his company. She could see why the women fell for him. He was charming with a capital C but he was most definitely not her type.

As they both had work in common, it was easy for her to steer the conversation around to the topic on everyone's lips—the death of the Foreign Minister of Tarparnii. Kim watched his facial expressions and mannerisms closely.

'What's your country like? I confess I've never been there but I'd love to hear all about it.'

Their coffees arrived and Kim slowly stirred hers as he talked.

'The beaches are the best the world has to offer, which is why we have such a wonderful tourist trade. The sunsets are more beautiful than here.' His rich accented voice held a hint of longing.

'You obviously miss it.'

'I do.'

'Do you have family there?'

'Yes. Except for my youngest sister, all my family are still there.'

'That must be worrying.' As he sipped at his coffee, Kim continued, 'I mean, with the state of political unrest sweeping through your country, surely it must be dangerous.'

'Every country has problems.' His tone was slightly defensive.

'I'm sorry, Ni. I wasn't criticising. I'm just trying to understand.'

'Why?'

Kim shrugged. 'Because I'm interested.' She looked coyly down at her cup before returning her gaze to meet his. 'It also gave me a reason to find the courage to ask you out.'

His smile was back in place and Kim returned it. 'I did something a bit stupid, actually.' She hesitated and then said, 'I did a bit of digging into the Foreign Minister's death.'

'Why?' he asked again, but his tone was much softer than last time.

Kim widened her eyes. 'I was in Theatre when he died. I'd been hoping for the chance to watch Dr Buchanan operate but I'd never expected him to lose his patient like that. It took all of us by surprise.'

'Not a lot surprises me any more.' He drank more of his coffee. 'Apparently the autopsy was performed this morning. I haven't heard any results.'

'Well, from where I was standing in Theatre, it looked like a heart attack.'

He shrugged. Interesting, Kim thought. A non-committal response. She waited, not daring to breathe a word. The silence reigned for a full minute and finally with a sense of triumph Kim saw his shoulders shrug once more.

'Appearances can be deceptive.'

'How so?' She frowned, hoping he wasn't talking about her.

He leaned forward and actually glanced around the room before saying in a stage whisper, 'Japarlin was going to be tried for crimes against my country on his return to Tarparnii.'

Kim leaned in closer. He had her full attention now. 'Do you agree with that?'

'Yes. He certainly deserved to be tried, but now Tarparniians don't have the satisfaction of seeing justice being done. It makes me wonder whether he was supposed to die here in Australia to save the faces of politicians back home.'

'A political stunt?'

'Something like that.'

'Who told you about it?'

'My father. He said there was even a report in the newspaper announcing that justice would be sought for the good of the country.'

'When did the report come out?'

'On Friday afternoon—Australian time.'

Kim's eyes widened. 'After the minister had already died,' she whispered. 'It's amazing.' She slowly sat back in her chair, shaking her head in wonder.

Ni took a deep breath and followed suit, picking up his cup and draining it. Kim's phone rang and she quickly excused herself to answer it.

'Where are you?' It was Tammy.

'I was just having a cup of coffee.'

'With Harry?'

'No. Do you need me back at the hospital?'

'Huh? Oh, yeah. Sure. We have a patient who needs a lobotomy to their patella.'

Kim tried not to smile but groaned instead. 'All right. Is the equipment ready?'

'Equipment? Are we doing reconnaissance tonight?'

'Yes. OK. I'll meet you there.'

'At your house?'

'Yes. I'm on my way already.'

'Now?' Tammy squeaked.

'Yes. Bye.' She disconnected the call.

'Duty calls.' Ni shrugged and paid for their drinks, waving away her effort to pay for her own coffee. 'Next time, you can buy.' He looked at her seductively and Kim couldn't help but smile.

'OK.' She hesitated a moment, then said, 'You're a nice man, Ni, and—'

'Nice? Oh, that's the kiss of death.'

She laughed. 'No, it's not.' They walked out of the coffee-shop together. 'You're just not my—'

'Not your type? No.' He nodded as though he agreed. 'Friends?'

'Definitely.'

He started walking off—thankfully in the opposite direction from the way she needed to go.

Kim managed to make it back to her apartment, shower and get changed for her date with Harry before Tammy turned up.

'Why didn't you return my calls?'

'No time. Harry's asked me to dinner and he's picking me up in…' she checked the clock on the wall '…ten minutes, and I still have to dry my hair. So let's run through everything in the bathroom.'

'I guess we're not having Chinese, then.'

'Sorry, Tam.'

'Who did you have coffee with?'

'Ni Kartu.'

'Good. Any interesting information?'

Kim relayed what she'd found out but Tammy didn't seem surprised. 'Moss told me about that in my meeting with him today.'

Kim switched off the hairdryer and quickly applied her make-up. 'What else did Moss say?'

'We have a full report of what was in the theatre bins. I've brought the list for you to have a look at to see if there's anything out of the ordinary.'

'Right, but basically…?'

'Everything looks fine but, then, you're the top medical expert.'

'OK. I'll take a look. Come and do my mascara because I always stuff it up.' Kim stood still while her friend helped her with her make-up. 'I'm getting my eyelashes tinted once this gig is up.'

'What's propofol?' Tammy asked as she finished one eye.

'It's a non-barbiturate hypnotic. It's an anaesthetic which is short-acting and has a brief sedative effect. It's usually used for short procedures. Why?'

'Because there were plenty of empty vials of it in those theatre bins.' Kim raised her eyebrows and Tammy scolded her. 'Keep still.'

'Sorry. Finished?'

'Yes.'

'Let's take a look at that list.' They headed out into the lounge room and Tammy pulled a file from her briefcase. Kim worked her way down the list.

'Is propofol bad?'

'Not at all, not if it's used the right way.' She shrugged. 'Same as any other drug. Misuse anything and it can be fatal.'

'So propofol's not something dangerous?'

'Well, it's not advised for people who are allergic to soybean and egg products but, as far as I know, the minister wasn't.'

'I'll check that out for you.'

'Thanks.' Kim flipped to the second page of the document and shook her head. 'There are way too many vials listed here for the operation.'

'How many extra?'

Kim sat down, reached for a pen and started to work it out. 'About seven 50-ml vials too many.'

'Would those extra vials trigger a heart attack?'

Kim smiled at her friend. 'They'd certainly kill the patient.'

'Bingo.'

'Bingo,' Kim repeated.

'Who was the anaesthetist again?'

'John McPhee.'

'OK. He's now top of the list.'

The doorbell rang and Kim checked the clock as she gathered up the papers and shoved them at Tammy. 'He's early.'

'Only by a few minutes.'

'Do I look all right?' she asked, fluffing her hands through her hair.

'Gorgeous. Make sure you wear your earpiece through dinner.' Tammy quickly handed Kim a small box which contained the subvocal earpiece before heading to the door.

'Sure. Anything else?' Kim put the earpiece in.

'Your skirt's back to front.'

Kim glanced down to discover her friend was right. 'Aaghh.' She switched her skirt around and shoved the empty box back into Tammy's bag.

'OK. Open the door,' she said nervously, smoothing a hand down her black A-line skirt which came to just above her knee.

'Hi, Harry. Come in,' Tammy said, and soon Harry was standing in front of her.

'Wow. You look lovely, Kimberlie.'

Kim couldn't help the smile that spread across her face. She glanced at him and realised he looked good enough to eat in a pair of black jeans, with a dark grey shirt opened to reveal the top of his chest. Kim had to stop herself from licking her lips. She met his gaze and although she knew she'd been caught checking him out again, this time she wasn't as embarrassed as before. This time, she wanted him to know just how much she appreciated him.

'Shoes would be good, though,' Tammy said into the silence that followed. Kim immediately broke her gaze from Harry's to stare down at her feet, almost amazed to find them still bare.

She laughed nervously. 'You've got a point there, Tam.' She smiled at Harry. 'Back in a second.' She raced to her room and did a twirl in front of the mirror, pleased with the way her burgundy top helped emphasise the good points of her figure and hide the bad ones. Slipping her feet into a pair of strappy sandals, she picked up her bag.

'Look, here she is,' Tammy announced.

'Ready.' She looked at Tammy. 'You'll lock up?'

'Sure. Go. Have a good time but not too late. You still have to *study*,' she said pointedly, meaning they desperately needed to finish talking about work.

'All right. All right. Quick.' Kim grabbed Harry's hand and tugged him out. 'Let's go before she changes her mind.' He smiled but didn't argue and bid a quick goodnight to Tammy.

Kim knew that as soon as they were out of sight, Tammy would need to get to the van downstairs to follow her to wherever they were going. When they reached Harry's car she stalled, saying she'd forgotten her keys, and rummaged through her small bag, looking for them. Out the corner of her eye she saw Tammy exit the building, and miraculously her key was found.

Harry drove them to a fashionable restaurant in the heart of Sydney which, she'd heard, was extremely difficult to get reservations at. 'I thought we weren't going anywhere special.' She glanced down at her skirt, feeling a little underdressed.

'You look incredible, Kimberlie. I'm trying to figure out how I'm going to keep my hands off you.'

She smiled shyly at him, deeply touched at the way he'd spoken. 'I'm sure you'll think of something.'

They were shown to their table by a snooty *maître d'* who fawned over Harry like he was royalty. After they'd ordered, Kim started to talk about the autopsy but Harry shook his head.

'Later,' was all he said as he reached across the table and took her hand in his. 'For a few hours, Kimberlie, let's just enjoy each other's company.'

'Like a *date*?'

A slow and sexy smile crossed his face and it was her undoing. Whenever he looked at her like that, the smile on his lips, his blue eyes mesmerising her, the warmth of his touch—it made her forget everything, and for the line of work she was in that definitely wasn't a good thing. Still, forgetting about everything wasn't totally bad so she decided to go with the flow and together they had a wonderful evening.

'Coffee?' he asked once they'd finished dessert.

Kim thought for a moment. 'I'm actually rather full. Would you mind if we have coffee back at your place?'

She watched as Harry's eyebrows hit his hair-line. 'No. Not at all.' He motioned for their waiter so he could take care of the bill.

'Nice going,' Tammy said in her ear. It had been so long since Tammy had said anything that Kim jumped.

'Kimberlie? What's wrong? Are you all right?'

She thought fast. Why would she be jumping for no reason? 'Er…hit my patella on the table leg.'

His smile replaced his concern as he came around the table. He gave her kneecap a little rub, the warmth of his touch sending shock waves throughout her body. Kim's eyes widened and she swallowed over her suddenly dry throat. 'Uh…it's fine now.' She was rewarded with another of his winning smiles, as though he knew exactly what his touch had done to her. He helped her up, continuing to hold her hand after she'd stood.

'Sorry about that,' Tammy said.

'I think I'll just visit the ladies' room before we leave. Won't be a moment.' She gave his hand a little squeeze before letting go.

'Nice going,' she muttered, as though talking to herself, and heard Tammy's laugh in response. 'Can't you keep quiet until you have something useful to say?' Her answer was another laugh from her friend. She refreshed her lipstick, fluffed her fingers through her hair and returned to find Harry waiting for her at the bar.

They drove home in silence but Harry had taken her hand in his after she'd returned from the ladies' room and hadn't let it go, except when he needed to turn corners, but even then once he'd finished, her hand was firmly back in his. It was a nice feeling and one she wouldn't mind experiencing day in, day out.

She glanced across at him, his profile flickering in the streetlights as he drove. Day in, day out? Had she just thought that? That was serious. She wasn't supposed to be thinking about things like that—like a long-term commitment or anything.

'Kimberlie.'

Even the way he said her name was like a caress.

'John McPhee's asked me to a party this Friday evening and I was wondering if you'd like to go along with me…as my date.'

Her first instinct was to say, Yes, yes, yes and…hmm let me think…yes! because it would be another date with Harry. The fact that it was to John McPhee's house was a bonus.

'Do it,' Tammy said in her ear.

'You don't have to answer right away.'

'I'd love to come,' she replied. 'Thank you for asking.' He pulled the car into the underground car park and turned to face her.

He released his seat belt. 'I'm glad you can accept.' He leaned forward and pressed his lips to hers. The pressure was soft and gentle, as though he'd been given a rare and precious gift and he wanted to treasure it for ever. How could a man make her feel that way just from a brief kiss?

He pulled back and looked at her, a slow smile spreading across his face, then cleared his throat before saying, 'Coffee.' He came around to open her door and the two of them headed inside.

Harry had been pleased when she'd suggested coffee back at his place, not only because it gave them an opportunity to talk about the autopsy but also because he planned on asking her some serious questions about who she really was. She'd become increasingly special to him in a short time yet he still felt as though he knew nothing about her. Tonight he was going to stop her from clamming up and he was going to get some answers...even if he had to coax them out of her with one round of kisses after another. He smiled to himself, looking forward to the prospect.

They were crossing the downstairs lobby where the security guard was located when Harry turned and spotted Mrs Pressman, his neighbour, getting out of a taxi. 'We'll wait for Mrs Pressman,' he said to Kim. 'That way, she doesn't have to wait for the lift to return.'

'Is she all right?' Kim watched as the elderly woman hobbled out of the taxi and closed the door. The taxi drove off as Mrs Pressman shifted her handbag onto her arm and put her walking stick on the ground.

'She has a bad leg. Ulcers.'

A second later a loud rumble, which sounded like a clap of thunder, ripped through the air. But it wasn't thunder. There wasn't any rain. As they stood there, Kim felt a prickle of apprehension wash over her. 'Something's wrong,' she whispered, and a moment later, there came the sound of glass shattering.

Harry and Kim rushed out of the lobby doors as glass and debris fell from the third floor of the heritage apartment building across the street. Flames licked out of a window and then receded, only to reappear a moment later. Mrs Pressman turned around at the sound of the noise and lost her footing, falling to the ground.

'Call the emergency services,' Harry ordered the security guard who had followed them outside, dropping Kim's hand and racing over to Mrs Pressman. 'Fire, police and ambulance.'

'Tammy?' Kim checked.

'What *was* that?' Tammy asked.

'Not sure. The building's on fire. It sounded like an explosion of some sort.'

CHAPTER SEVEN

KIM had been in several situations over the years when she'd been required to think fast on her feet, yet tonight her first thought was not about in what order she should do things but her concern for Harry as he rushed out to help. What if there was another explosion? What if he was hurt?

Kim knew she had to push those thoughts away, compartmentalise them and let them out later when things were under control, but old memories started resurfacing without permission. She glanced back at Clarry, who'd gone as white as a sheet before rushing inside to do as Harry had instructed.

She continued to scan the area, looking for anything that seemed suspicious. 'Tammy? You there?'

'Yes. I'm just pulling up now. Wow. What a mess. Do you want me to call it in?'

'Security at Harry's apartment's already doing that.' She headed over to where Harry was crouched beside Mrs Pressman. 'Everything all right?'

'I'm fine, dear,' Mrs Pressman answered.

'Who were you talking to?' Harry queried, but didn't look up.

'Just prioritising.'

'Good. Stay here with Mrs Pressman and check her hip for me.'

'I'm fine, boy. Stop fussing.' But even as Mrs Pressman spoke, she winced with pain when Kim touched her hip.

'Doesn't feel dislocated but the NOF may be fractured.'

'The *NOF*?' Mrs Pressman said the letters as if they were disgusting.

'Neck of femur,' Harry supplied, as he stood up and headed across the street.

'Where are you going?' Kim demanded, her eyes wide with fear.

'To help.'

'Harry, the third floor is on fire!' She could feel the hysteria beginning to rise. He couldn't go in there. He just couldn't. She had to stop him. 'Harry. No. Wait. You can't go in there. You might get hurt.'

Harry was a little puzzled at her reaction. 'It's fine, Kimberlie. I know what I'm doing.' He wasn't standing around to argue and she watched in horror as he disappeared inside the building. Nausea and panic rose within her and she gasped for air. Her heart was in her throat as she glanced up at the flames licking out from the third-floor window. This wasn't happening. It couldn't happen—not again. She needed him.

'Kim? Kim?' Tammy's voice came through her earpiece. 'Kim, what's going on?'

'Harry's gone inside,' she said wildly, her mind a confused jumble of overwhelming emotions.

'I know, dear,' Mrs Pressman answered. 'He's a brave boy and doesn't take uncalculated risks. He'll be all right.'

Clarry came out of the apartment block. 'The emergency crews are on their way.'

'Kim?' Tammy's voice was firm. 'Concentrate. I need you to concentrate.'

Kim forced herself to look away from the building, to focus on the people around her. 'Clarry, get some blankets for Mrs Pressman. She's not to be moved until the paramedics arrive. Also, you're in charge of crowd control until the cavalry gets here.'

Clarry stood to attention. 'Right.'

'I'm…umm…' Kim straightened, her mouth dry. She rubbed a hand down her skirt. 'I'm going to…uh…go in and help Harry.' She handed Clarry her bag. 'Hold this, please.' She set off before she could change her mind or before she started thinking about things too closely.

'Kim? You don't have to do this,' Tammy said.

'Yes, I do. I'm not going to lose him. I need him, Tammy.' Her heart was thumping so violently against her chest the sound reverberated in her ears. Her palms were wet with perspiration and she hadn't gone anywhere near the fire yet. She stopped just outside the entrance to the building, closed her eyes and ran through some cognitive therapy exercises her psychologist had taught her years back.

'Kim?'

'I'm OK, Tam.' She opened her eyes and let out a large breath, forcing herself to calm right down before heading in. She focused on the anger now surging through her. How dared Harry just walk off like that—into a burning building? Didn't he realise he could get hurt? Didn't he realise there were people out here who needed him? She clenched her jaw and focused on her task.

'You be careful and keep in contact.'

The stairs weren't situated in a stairwell as they would have been in a new building. Instead, they ran along the inside side wall of the building, the rails made out of lovely old wood which would combust so easily it made Kim shudder. As she walked up the stairs, people were still standing around their open apartment doors, unsure what was happening.

'There's a fire in the building,' she said, her voice carrying authority. 'Evacuate in a calm manner.' She headed over to the fire alarm on the wall, took off her shoe and broke the glass so she could press the button. Where was Harry? Why hadn't he raised the alarm? Was he all right? Had he been knocked unconscious? Panic started to rise in her chest as her mind went into overdrive. She headed up the stairs to the second floor.

As she came to the landing to the second floor, she saw people coming out of their apartments, some concerned, some hysterical and others just plain confused. 'Don't take the lift,' Kim warned. 'Head down the stairs. The emergency services will be here soon. Don't panic,' she said to a hysterical woman who was sobbing. 'Are you hurt?'

'No.'

'Is anyone else in your apartment?'

'No b-but the loud noises…they set my heart racing and I can't stop it. I can't breathe.' The woman's eyes were wide with unrepressed fear.

'What's your name?'

'Enid.'

'Hi, Enid. I'm Kim and I'm a doctor.' Kim placed her hand on Enid's wrist, feeling her pulse. It was fast and thready. She needed to calm down, stat. 'Enid, all you need to do is slowly make your way down the stairs. There are personnel down there waiting to help you.' Kim grabbed the arm of a young man who was about to head down the stairs. 'What's your name?'

'Jamie.'

'Jamie, would you mind escorting Enid down the stairs, please?'

'Sure.'

'You'll be fine,' Kim reassured Enid.

'Aren't you coming down, dear?'

'I'm going up to check out the top floor.'

'You be careful, dear,' Enid said, and her concern for Kim was touching. It also showed that Enid was starting to calm down if she could think about something other than her own situation.

Smoke was starting to come down the stairs as Kim headed up to the third floor. The lurid stench filling her nostrils made her want to gag. This wasn't the same. This wasn't how it had been four years ago when Chris had died. The words kept repeating themselves over and over in her head as she took step after step up towards where she knew Harry had gone.

'Harry?' she called, but received no reply. A bubble of panic rose again and she hiccuped in horror.

'Kim? What's wrong?' Tammy asked.

'I can't find him. Harry!' She called louder and coughed as she breathed in too much smoke.

'Kimberlie. Over here.'

Relief burst the bubble and she followed the sound of his voice, reaching her hands out in front of her as the dark plumes of smoke became thicker.

'Stay low,' he called, and as his words penetrated her fuzzy mind, she remembered her training and immediately crouched down on all fours.

'Why didn't I wear trousers?' she muttered.

'Hear those sirens, Kim?' Tammy said. 'Fire brigade is just pulling up.'

'Fire brigade's here,' Kim said to Harry.

'Good. Over here, keep coming. When I first came up here, the smoke wasn't that bad. All the apartments on this floor have been evacuated except for this one, which is where the smoke is coming from.'

'The fire brigade's here. Let's wait for them to come up and break the door down.'

'Briefing them now,' Tammy said. Kim reached out and felt Harry's hand. He hauled her to him and cradled her momentarily in his arms.

Kim clung to him, overwhelmed with relief that he was all right.

'Don't you ever go into a fire-riddled building again,' she warned him crossly. 'I wouldn't survive the shock.'

Harry noted the strain in her voice and how it had trembled when she'd called his name before. This wasn't how he'd expected Kimberlie to react. He'd expected her to be as gung-ho about helping as she was about everything else she did. He tightened his hold on her. She was acting strangely, which meant something wasn't right.

'Fire brigade are on their way up. Where are you?' Tammy asked.

'Sitting on the floor outside a third-floor apartment with smoke billowing around us isn't my idea of fun,' she said conversationally, giving Tammy the information she'd requested.

'If the firefighters don't get up here soon, we're going to have to break this door in. There are obviously people in this apartment and it frustrates me not to be able to help them.'

The sound of footsteps in the stairwell was the answer to her prayers. 'Dr Buchanan? Dr Mason?'

'Over here,' Harry called. 'Clarry must have told them we were in here,' he reasoned. 'The smoke is coming from this apartment. The door's stuck. Have you got a first-aid kit?'

The firefighters reached them and handed them both gas masks. 'Yes. Put these on and move away so we can break the door down.' Kim allowed Harry to move her to the side as the firefighters did their job.

Kim cringed and buried her head against Harry as they broke down the door, hoses at the ready. She couldn't look. The smell and the sounds were bad enough and she didn't know how she was going to be able to concentrate on anyone they found in the apartment.

She began shaking and Harry was instantly concerned. 'Kimberlie?' It was hard to understand each other with the masks on, but she recognised her name on his lips. Her answer was to hold him tighter. She didn't want to let him go. She'd ordered Chris not to go but she hadn't stopped him as he'd rushed into a burning building—only to have him never return.

It had taken her years to be this comfortable with a man, a man who was currently surpassing all her expectations, and she realised in that one moment that she loved him. She loved Harry! She honestly loved this man who was holding her so completely against him. She'd investigated him, she'd lied to him, yet she loved him. She closed her eyes and despised the world she was living in. How could she continue lying to the man she loved? It was impossible.

'How are things going, Kim?' Tammy's voice came through.

'Terrible,' she mumbled.

'I can hardly hear you but at least I know you're still alive and kicking. Just remember to take deep breaths. This isn't the same situation, Kim. The firefighters are here and both you and Harry are fine. You need to focus on the patients, Kim. This is what you're trained to do. Let the firefighters take care of the fire while you and Harry take care of the patients. At the moment you're a doctor first and foremost, so push everything else to the back of your mind, the panic, the worry. Leave it all behind, Kim, and concentrate.'

Yes, she had to concentrate. She raised her head and immediately felt Harry's arms loosening. She looked up at him but it was hard, not only with the masks on but because of the smoke surrounding them. At least she was no longer having to choke in breath after breath. She peered through the mask, met his gaze and saw what she needed—reassurance.

Kim took a soothing breath and turned to watch what the firefighters were doing. They were still bringing the fire under control and although it had seemed like ages since she'd been there in Harry's arms, it had, in reality, been only a minute or two. Why was it that when things were going badly, time seemed to stand still so you could absorb all the horrible things around you?

'Over here,' a firefighter called. On a blanket, they dragged a teenage girl. 'Fire looks to have started in a gas oven but we're getting it under control. Chances are there's another person in there. This one's all yours.'

Thankfully, the dense smoke had started to lift and Kim focused on the girl they'd dragged out into the hallway. One of the firefighters was attaching a gas mask to the girl's face. 'She's going to need oxygen,' Kim said, to Harry and he nodded. They crouched down, one on either side of her, and Harry opened the first-aid kit.

The girl had several lacerations across her arms, face and legs and one across her back, but none of them were life-threatening. He took her pulse and found it slow. He pulled out a stethoscope from the kit and listened to her heartbeat. Her lungs sounded tight but he knew it could be fixed as soon as she received oxygen.

'Looks as though she's fractured or dislocated her shoulder,' Kim said, after she'd felt the girl's arms and legs. 'She'll need X-rays and it will be better if she's taken out of here via stretcher.'

'Copy that,' Tammy said.

'Agreed.' Harry nodded. 'Let's move her closer to the stairs and then we can ask the fire-fighters to call down for a stretcher.' They shifted the girl along on the blanket, being careful of the fire hoses as well as the patient's injuries. Half a minute passed before paramedics, complete with gas masks, came up the stairs.

'Wow. These guys are really reading our minds tonight,' Harry said. They carefully transferred the girl to the stretcher and, after giving the paramedics orders and asking them to send up another stretcher, let them carry her out of the building.

It was only a moment later the firefighters called out that they'd found another woman. She was also carried out on a blanket and placed before Harry and Kim. She, too, was unconscious but her face, arms and hands were badly burnt. She also had half a dinner plate sticking out of her abdomen.

'We need to get her out,' Harry said. He pulled on a fresh pair of gloves and pressed his fingers to the woman's pulse. 'Not good. Oxy-viva. Plasma and saline, stat.'

'Plasma and saline, stat, oxygen, stat,' Kim repeated. 'We need that stretcher now!' The urgency in her voice could be unsurpassed, and once more a stretcher appeared. With the help of the paramedics, they lifted the woman up on the blanket and transferred her to the stretcher.

'Anyone else?' Harry asked one of the firefighters.

'Not that we can see.'

'This woman requires our urgent attention so we're going down.'

'Copy that. We'll continue cleaning up this mess. Fire's under control but we need to make sure everything's damped down.'

The paramedics were already on their way down with the patient and Harry and Kim made their way over to the stairs and began descending.

'Are you all right, Kimberlie?' Harry said as they reached the first floor landing. There was smoke everywhere now but at least down here it was much thinner.

'Yes.' As they headed outside, she took off her mask, handing it to a policeman. Harry followed suit and together they climbed into the back of the ambulance with the woman. As the doors closed, Kim caught a glimpse of Tammy giving her the thumbs-up sign.

'You head on to the hospital,' Tammy said. 'I'll pick up communication with you once you're out of Theatre.' There was a click and Kim knew Tammy had terminated their connection.

She focused on their patient and as the ambulance started to move off, Kim and Harry were hard at work, taking the gas mask off their patient and replacing it with oxygen, rigging up a saline drip and plasma. Kim checked the woman's pulse.

'It's not good, Harry. It's not strong enough.'

Harry was taking a closer look at the woman's abdomen. 'She has too much internal bleeding,' he said, changing the gauze pad.

'Do you think it's gone through her large and small intestines and maybe even pierced the stomach wall?'

He shrugged. 'That explosion was pretty powerful.' They pulled up at the hospital and the paramedics opened the rear doors. 'Take her straight through to Theatre. I need at least two units of blood, get the ortho and plastic surgeons here immediately. Kimberlie, once you've handed over to the theatre staff, go and scrub.' With that, Harry walked off, pulling his bloodied gloves from his hands, folding them together and tossing them in the appropriate bin as he walked through to emergency Theatres.

Jerry came up and walked beside him. 'Isn't it your night off?'

'Kimberlie and I were the first medics on site. I'll take this woman through to surgery. Join us if you like.'

'Do you think Kim will be able to handle assisting you by herself?'

Harry entered the male changing rooms. 'She'll be fine. She's a natural when it comes to surgery, that much I've noted.' As they spoke, Harry continued getting ready.

'So have I.' Jerry watched Harry closely. 'You think she's had more training than we've been told.' It was a statement.

'Yes.' He paused for a split second and frowned before shaking his head. 'Anyway, it's to our advantage.'

'True. OK. I'll let you get on with it.'

'Oh, Jerry.' Harry called his registrar back. 'Do me a favour and find out about Mrs Pressman. She's my neighbour and should have been brought in or be on her way in with a possible fractured hip. Make sure those orthopods take care of her and give me a progress report when you can.'

'Consider it done.'

Harry had almost finished scrubbing when Kimberlie joined him at the sink.

'Blood transfusion is under way and her BP is slowly looking up. Plastics and ortho—both notified. Second saline bag has been started. Radiographs are being processed and should be here soon.'

'Good.' He headed off to gown up and soon Kim followed him. After debriding the wound and with the bright theatre lights above, Harry was able to see the damage more clearly.

Kim held the retractors, passed him the suction and had the sutures ready when he needed them. Harry performed the surgery in a methodical way, taking each organ in turn and making sure everything was perfect before moving on to the next.

'You are a real natural with surgery,' he remarked when she pre-empted him once more. 'You've definitely chosen the right profession.'

Kim smiled, even though he wouldn't be able to see it behind her mask. She glanced up and met his gaze and could see he was impressed. His praise made her feel incredible and she realised that right at that moment she'd found fulfillment in her professional life. Never before had she received so much support and encouragement from anyone—even when she'd been training—

and just for a moment she wished that she *was* a service registrar under Harry's guidance. The fact this praise had come from the man she loved was a bonus.

Jerry came into surgery two hours after they'd started. He'd stood there watching for a while before Harry said, 'I don't need you, Jerry. Kimberlie's doing a superb job of assisting so I guess you can go catch up on some paperwork.'

'Oh, great,' Jerry said flatly. 'How I love paperwork.'

'Don't we all.' Harry chuckled. 'Anything to report on Mrs Pressman?'

'Yes. She's had her scans, the hip is fractured and she'll probably need a total hip replacement.'

'Which surgeon is she under?'

'Head of unit.'

Harry glanced up at his registrar. 'Thank you. I appreciate you taking care of that for me.'

'No problem. She's a nice lady.'

'Yes she is. Suction.' Jerry left them in peace. Once they had installed the necessary drains and done yet another check X-ray to make sure everything was where it should be, Harry was satisfied and ready to hand over to the orthopaedic and plastic surgeons. Both registrars had been in to have a look at the patient earlier on but they hadn't been able to do anything until the patient had been stabilised.

'She's all yours,' Harry said, stepping back from the table and ripping off his gloves. Kim degowned as well and as they walked out Harry stretched his arms above his head. 'I definitely need that cup of coffee we'd planned on having.' He glanced at Kimberlie and felt desire rumble deep in his gut as he realised she was watching him with hungry eyes as he stretched, his theatre trousers dipping slightly.

He leaned over, first to one side, then the other, stretching out his obliques, enjoying the way her gaze seemed to be devouring him. Finally, he dropped his hands and she sighed, raising her eyes to meet his.

When she realised he'd been conscious of her appraisal, she closed her eyes in embarrassment. 'Sorry,' she muttered. 'You keep catching me staring at you.' Her words were met by a deep chuckle.

'Hey, don't apologise. You enjoyed it and so did I.' He took her hand in his and gave it a squeeze. 'Coffee. Definitely coffee. Let's go see what the cafeteria has to offer at this hour of the night…or, rather, morning.'

Harry didn't let go of her hand as they walked through the busy A and E department, taking a shortcut towards the cafeteria. Was he mad, or just tired with fatigue? Thankfully, there weren't as many people around during the night shift as there were during the day but still she could feel all eyes on them as they walked along. It wasn't that she didn't *like* him holding her hand, quite the opposite. It was just that she was so conscious of this public display of affection and, regardless of how few people were working, it only took one to spread the gossip that she and Harry were an item.

Were they? She hardly knew herself, even though she desperately wanted it. There was too much to sort out between them, and once Harry learned of her deception, even though it was a good cause, she doubted he'd want to speak with her again. She gave his hand a little squeeze, eager to have this moment to file away in her memory banks because she knew her life would fall apart when she told him the truth.

Thankfully, the café was all but deserted and after they'd helped themselves to coffee, Kim sat opposite Harry, the table between them. She glanced down into her cup, her heart starting to beat wildly against her ribs as she contemplated telling him the truth. She was glad he was off the suspect list regarding Mr Japarlin's death, knowing, as she had all along, that Harry was a decent, honest, hard-working man. She didn't deserve him. Still…she had to hope.

If she uttered a word about her real job, she'd be breaking her cover without authorisation and would get into a lot of trouble. Was it worth it? Was *he* worth it? She ran her finger around the edge of her coffee-cup, deep in thought as she imagined how he would react if she told him she loved him. Surely that wasn't going against the rules?

Harry, I know we haven't known each other very long but tonight when we were sitting in that smoke-filled building, I realised I was in love with you. Hope you don't mind.

No. It wouldn't do. That wasn't the way you told someone you loved them. It had to be perfect, not over a cup of coffee in the hospital cafeteria after they'd had a long session in Theatre.

'Why don't you like fires?'

Kim was startled at the sound of his voice and spilt her coffee over her hands. Harry snatched up some napkins and patted her hands dry before mopping up the spilt liquid from the table.

'I'm beginning to think you should start drinking iced coffee—preferably from a carton so it's not as easy to spill.' He chuckled as he checked her hands to make sure she hadn't scalded herself.

Kim closed her eyes at his gentle touch and sighed. When she finally opened them again, it was to find him looking at her with a sense of wonder. It was as though he'd unwrapped a beautiful new gift and wasn't quite sure what to do with it. Unfortunately for him, he still had a few more layers to unwrap. Kim pushed that thought from her mind and cleared her throat.

'Why don't I like fires?' She repeated his earlier question, knowing he had every right to an answer. She'd have to be careful how she answered but he deserved as much truth from her as she was allowed to give. 'My fiancé died in one.'

CHAPTER EIGHT

'YOU were engaged? When?'

Kim half expected Harry to pull his hand away, to withdraw, but, as though she were being handed a miracle, he didn't.

'Four years ago. Chris and I met through work and within a week or two were engaged.' She shrugged. 'Things seem to happen quickly for me. Always have.' She sighed and took a deep breath. 'We were overseas working in Papua New Guinea and had just finished a stint in—' She broke off, correcting herself. 'Just finished a shift. We were walking to a friend's place when two houses were firebombed.' Kim paused, unable to meet Harry's gaze. 'It was a time of unrest in that country,' she explained and then closed her eyes. That was a mistake because the scene replayed so vividly in her mind that she could smell the stench, feel the flames and hear the cries of the people.

She felt Harry squeeze her hand and realised she'd spoken out loud. 'He just went in, saying he had to help them. I ordered him not to but he didn't listen.'

'Ordered?'

'You know,' she corrected. 'Told him, begged him, but he didn't consider the danger to himself and I admit when I realised he wasn't coming out, *I* wanted to go in and drag him out, but by then a few colleagues were there and held me back.'

Kim slowly opened her eyes and gazed at the man opposite her. Her vision was blurred because of the tears which had started to slip silently down her face. Harry reached out and brushed them away tenderly.

'And tonight I just rushed in. No wonder you were upset but, believe me, Kimberlie, had there been any danger to me, I would have waited. At least the building was evacuated without anyone else being seriously hurt.'

Kim paused, brushing tears away with her free hand. 'Why didn't you break the fire alarm and set it off?'

'I did. On the ground floor. When I didn't hear any bells ringing, I thought it was a new silent alarm. Then, later, I heard the alarm and realised it hadn't been triggered properly.' He paused. 'You thought something had happened to me?'

'Yes.'

'Because I hadn't raised the alarm, you thought I was hurt.' He nodded as though things finally made sense.

'Yes.'

Harry stood, not letting go of her hand, and came around the table to sit next to her. Kim shifted in her chair so she was facing him. 'And you still came into the building to look for me. That was very brave of you, Kimberlie.'

'I've been trained to be brave.' The words came out before she could stop them. Quickly, she continued. 'It's all part of being a doctor. We see things that aren't nice, we help out where we can. I'll admit I can stand almost anything… except fires.'

'Thank you for sharing that with me. I know how hard that must have been, but I appreciate it more than I can say.' Gently, he slipped his hand from hers, trailing his fingers over her palm. Shifting even closer, he brushed her hair back from her face, caressing her skin. 'You've become special to me, Kimberlie,' he murmured as he tenderly cupped her face. His heart was beating an unsteady tattoo and he wasn't used to feeling so helpless where a woman was concerned, yet that was exactly how she made him feel.

He brushed his thumb over her lips and they instinctively parted as she sucked in a breath.

'You've knocked me completely off balance,' he continued. 'And I quite like it.' His smile was small…but, as far as she was concerned, it was deadly. When he looked at her like that, with tenderness and caring and giving and sharing, it tore her in two. She desperately wanted to accept everything he was offering and the fact that she couldn't… She pushed the thought away and focused on the touch of his thumb on her lips, the way a light tingle was spreading throughout her body as though it were the base for the excitement she knew would spread so easily within her…all from his simple touch.

His mouth was almost on top of hers, she could feel his breath against her parted lips and it was pure, sweet agony. Her brain had shut down, only concentrating on the small space which still separated them.

'Kimberlie.' He groaned her name as though the torture he was putting them both through was too much, and in the next instant his mouth was firmly pressed on hers. She sighed and leaned into him, wanting him to deepen the kiss, to have more of the passion they'd only glimpsed the last time they'd kissed. Instead, he kept it light, soft and, oh so sexy. Never before had she felt so alive from such a gentle touch.

'OK, honestly, if you two don't want to be gossiped about, you're going to have to stop doing these things in such public places.' Jerry's voice cut into their own personal world like a scalpel.

Kim jerked backwards a little but Harry, ignoring his registrar, finished what he'd started and, after running his fingers through her hair, eventually turned to face the source of the interruption.

'What's up, Jerry?'

'Multiple trauma. The ortho boys are having a look now but there are a few patients who'll be needing our attention. I know you two aren't on duty, but we're not coping up there. Is there any chance…?'

'Duty calls.' Harry stood and pulled Kim to her feet. He gave her hand a squeeze before bringing it to his lips. Ignoring Jerry, he said, 'Thank you.' That was all he needed to say—his eyes conveyed the rest. He pressed his lips against her hand before smiling and leading the way out into the corridor.

As they headed back towards A and E, Harry asked Jerry, 'How's our fire patient doing?'

'Still in Theatre with the burns specialist.'

'Do we have a name for her yet?'

'Louanne Curruthers. Forty-seven years old. Daughter's name is Cynthia.'

'Make sure she has access to her mother once Louanne's out of Recovery. Usual ICU visiting, but I don't want Cynthia caught up in the hospital system, wondering where her mother is.'

'I'll take care of it.' Jerry nodded.

'Any word on how the fire started?'

'Yes. The firefighters found a blackened-to-a-crisp…thing in the oven. Someone said it looked like a meringue or pavlova, or at least that's what they think it was. Apparently, you need to cook pavlova in a coolish oven and sometimes with a gas oven, if you turn it down too low, the flame can go out. They also take quite a few hours to bake.'

Kim raised her eyebrows. 'Well, Jerry, aren't you the domesticated one.'

'Er…my Aunt Harriet likes to cook and she's had the same trouble with the gas oven when she's been making meringues.'

'So they put the pavlova on to bake, the flame goes out, the gas is still coming out, the gas then builds up, so when she opened the oven… How did it catch alight?'

'Louanne's a smoker.'

'Ah. That'll do it. Then we have a fire flame which shoots straight into the apartment, shattering windows, causing drapes, cushion fabrics, whatever, to ignite and, *voilà*, we have a fire.'

Kimberlie shuddered and Harry placed his hand on her shoulder. 'Sorry,' he said softly.

'It's OK.' They walked down the stairwell and came out near A and E. 'So, what's first up?' She schooled her thoughts, focusing on what was needed.

'Examination cubicles 2 and 4 for you.' Jerry handed her the patient files. 'Trauma room 1 for you.' He gave Harry a file. 'And I'll take examination cubicles 3, 5 and 9.'

The instant Harry accepted the file, she could tell he was in full doctor mode. He'd pushed everything else, herself included, into little pigeonholes in his mind. She did the same and headed off to check her patients.

When she pulled back the curtain for cubicle two it was to find a man in his late twenties sitting up on the bed. He had green and red spiky hair she was sure she could cut her fingers on, piercings in his ears, nose, eyebrows and lip, tattoos on his arms and chest. But the thing that brought a smile of incredulity to her face was the fact that he had headphones on, blaring loud music, and was air-drumming, his eyes closed in complete concentration. The bed sheet was pulled up just past his groin and one hairy leg was sticking out the end with a thick sock covering his foot.

She noticed the white bandage the A and E doctors had put on his abdomen until she could come take a closer look. Kim read the notes and raised her eyebrows at what was written there. Closing the file once more, she placed it on a side table and walked over to the bed.

'Er…Switch?'

No answer, just more air-drumming, with vigour.

Kim reached out and tapped him on the shoulder. He yelled in fright and Kim couldn't stop the scream that came from her lips as he, in turn, scared her as well.

'Sorry,' she said, nervous laughter taking over.

'Ow.' Switch placed one hand on his abdomen and took off his headphones with the other.

'Sorry,' Kim said again, and almost jumped out of her skin when the curtain to the cubicle was wrenched open and Harry and two nurses came in.

Harry took one look at the patient and crossed to Kim's side, standing slightly in front of her in a protective manner. 'What's going on in here?'

'Nothing. Harry, it's all right. Mr… er…Switch had his headphones on and I'm afraid I startled him.' Kim put her hand on

Harry's shoulder, gently putting pressure on him to move away. 'Then he startled me and, well, you know how jumpy I am. It's OK. I'm OK.'

He glanced at her and she nodded reassuringly. Harry turned to one of the nurses. 'Sister will assist you, Dr Mason.'

'Thank you.' Her smile was genuine and bright. Harry stood in the doorway. 'It's fine, Harry. Go,' she added, when it didn't seem as though he was going to move. He looked at Switch and then nodded before pulling the curtain shut after him.

'Boyfriend?' Switch asked.

Kim just laughed. 'What seems to be the trouble, Switch?'

'I thought it was written down in the notes?'

'It is and I've read them, but it also helps if you can tell me.'

'Why?'

'To check your mental clarity. The notes tell me you were involved in a bar fight and were, among other things, hit over the head with a bottle.'

'Uh, sure, but that's happened before so it's no biggy.' He pointed to his stomach. 'It's this.'

Kim gingerly lifted the bandage and her eyes widened. There, lodged in his stomach, was the top of a drumstick. 'Have you been given anything for the pain?'

'Nah. Don't need it.' He lifted his headphones. 'Music's my main relaxant. Always destresses me. Besides, I've had a few drinks tonight so I guess it's best not to give me anything anyway.'

'You have no pain?'

'Well…yeah, it hurts if I move suddenly…like if someone was to scare me or something.' He grinned at Kim and she smiled back.

'Let's not do that again.' She turned to the sister. 'X-rays?'

'Here, Dr Mason.' She hooked them onto the viewing machine and Kim shook her head in wonder.

'You've somehow managed to avoid everything you should have avoided.'

'Terrific. I'll tell the bloke who stabbed me that he did a good job.' Switch laughed. 'Let me know when you're ready, Doc, and I'll get into the zone.' He lifted the headphones onto his ears but didn't press the play button on his CD player.

'All righty, then.' Kim turned to the sister. 'I'll give Switch a local, then we'll debride, and once we've removed the stick, we'll give him a wicked stitching job and a lovely sterile bandage.'

The sister smiled and nodded before getting the equipment they'd need out of the cupboards. When Kim was ready to administer the local, Switch blasted his ears with loud, heavy metal music, watching as the needle was put in. Once she was done, he started air-drumming again, closing his eyes, and she marvelled at the control he had over his pain threshold.

She had to wait for a break between songs, not wanting to startle him again, to let him know she was ready to proceed. Switch nodded, turned the volume control up even more—which Kim had thought impossible—and signalled for her to go on. Once more he watched everything she did, from how she draped his abdomen around the wound site to how she gently and carefully removed the top end of the stick, ensuring none of it splintered.

When she held it up for his approval he nodded, closed his eyes and started his drumming once more. Kim, completely proud of herself, placed the foreign object into a kidney dish and began making sure there was nothing else left behind before she sutured the wound closed.

'Find a jar for that,' she said to the sister. 'Something tells me Switch is going to want that as a souvenir.' Kim tidied the area and wrote up her notes. When the song ended, she called her patient's name and he switched off the music.

'Everything done?' He looked down in surprise at the nice white bandage she'd put on him.

'All fixed.'

'Good job. Can I go?'

'No. I'd like you stay for the next hour at least, just so we can monitor you.'

'Nah. I'll be fine.'

'Please? It'll put my mind at rest.'

He looked at her and then nodded. 'OK, but only for you.'

'Good. If I'm not in Theatre, I'll come back and see you.'

'Cool. Hey, listen, if you ever want to go for a night out, come down to the club in King's Cross.' He named a popular bar she'd heard of but had never frequented. 'The music's good and the area's not really as scary as people might think. Besides, I'm a legend on the drums. Crazy Shadows—that's the name of my band. We rock!'

Kim nearly choked on her tongue. 'You're the drummer for Crazy Shadows?'

'Yeah. Why? Have you heard of us?'

They were Tammy's all-time favourite band and she knew her friend would go ballistic when she discovered Kim had treated the drummer. 'My friend is a big fan.'

'Excellent. Then make sure you pay us a visit.'

Kim inclined her head and looked at him questioningly. 'How many beers did you have tonight, Switch?'

He frowned and then rolled his eyes, sighing. 'Three—but don't tell the guys, OK? They think I can drink like a fish but there's no way I can drum when I'm slobbering drunk.'

She laughed. 'And I'll bet you had those beers earlier on in the night.'

'You guessed it, Doc.'

'It's amazing that your music helps you so much. I'm impressed.'

Switch merely shrugged and glanced behind her. Kim turned to find Harry standing in the doorway, the curtain closed behind him. 'Hi. Switch, here, is the drummer for Crazy Shadows.'

'That's great,' Harry said dryly. 'All finished here?'

'Yes.'

'I was asked to give you this.' He held up the jar containing the remainder of the drumstick.

Kim smiled as she took it from him. 'Thanks.' She turned to Switch. 'I thought you'd like to keep this.'

'Excellent.'

'Well, if I can get back to see you, I will, but otherwise take care and make sure you take some analgesics if you need to.'

He shrugged noncommittally. 'You try and get down to the bar to check us out.'

'Once I tell Tammy I treated you, she'll hardly let me stay away.'

'Tammy? Your friend is Tammy? Short blonde hair, brown eyes?' His eyes were wide with astonishment.

Kim frowned and looked at Harry then back to Switch. 'You know her?'

'Yep. Tam's a hotty. Hasn't been to the bar much lately. She's got some weird job which means she works strange hours.'

'Yes, she does.' Kim nodded. 'Anyway, I have more patients to see.'

'OK. Thanks, Doc.' He motioned to Harry. 'You've got quite a girl there, mate. Hang onto her.'

Harry nodded. 'I'll do my best.' They walked out of the cubicle and Kim returned the notes to the nurses' station. 'I need you in Theatre,' he said.

'I have a patient in cubicle 4 to see.'

'That's why I need you in Theatre. Gallstones. Patient's been in several times with gallstone-related pain. Twice we've been able to use ultrasonic lithotripsy to break the stones down so they're small enough to pass naturally. This time the pain's much worse. You were busy removing drumsticks so Jerry took a look at the patient. The CT scan showed larger stones and the gall bladder has suffered a lot of scar tissue.'

'Cholecystectomy?'

Harry nodded. 'Jerry and I think so.'

'You don't want to try lithotripsy once more?'

'No time. Patient's already in pre-med. I thought perhaps you'd like to do the surgery as you've probably observed quite a few and via laparoscopy it's not that difficult.'

'OK. I'll give it a go.'

'I'm sure you will.' He frowned for a second and then looked at her closely. 'Switch, eh?'

Kim smiled as they walked towards emergency Theatres. 'He's a nice guy.'

'Not your type?'

Her smile increased. Did all men think the word 'nice' was the kiss of death as far as relationships went? 'Fishing?'

Harry stopped outside the changing rooms. 'Maybe.' His smile was slow and sexy and Kim melted right there and then.

'I'll bite.' She couldn't control the butterflies in her stomach or the way her knees went weak or the way her breathing became shallow or the way this man made her feel!

'Good.' He raised his eyebrows suggestively and Kim nearly choked on her tongue. With that, Harry turned and headed into the changing rooms, leaving her standing there staring at the door.

Kim found it difficult to control her thoughts as she stood by the scrub sink with Harry. He was too close and she could almost feel the warmth emanating from his body. The scent of him, which she was completely addicted to, was winding itself around her, drugging her senses. If she looked up and met his deep, blue gaze, she'd end up being a messy puddle on the floor.

She concentrated on scrubbing. This was no way to prepare for Theatre. Harry was more than happy to stay with her and Jerry returned to A and E as he was the registrar on call for the general surgical department.

'What happened with that MVA Jerry wanted you to look at?' she asked, forcing her mind into medical gear.

'Patient has minimal abdominal injuries but a fractured femur. The orthopaedic boys have taken her to Theatre to stabilise the femoral artery and once they're done, they'll page Jerry.' Harry waited until Kim's gaze met his. 'Ready?'

'Yes.'

Kim went into Theatre, surprised she was feeling a little nervous having Harry watching her. She'd done this operation hundreds of times before so why on earth should this one be any different?

Once the patient was ready, she made a one-centimetre puncture just above the umbilicus and inflated the abdominal cavity with carbon dioxide to improve her visibility. She inserted the laparoscope, which had a camera attached, into the abdomen. Two more punctures were needed just below the ribs for the grasping forceps. Just to the right of the midsection, she made a fourth puncture to insert the dissection laser.

Glancing up at Harry, she realised she'd made the mistake of not asking his advice on anything she'd just done. Oh, well, too late now. She had an operation to perform. Watching carefully on the closed-circuit monitors, she retracted then dissected the gall bladder, grasping it with the forceps so she could remove it.

'Well done.' Harry's voice was firm and businesslike. Kim completed the procedure and wrote up the operation notes, ordering IV antibiotics for the patient.

As they degowned and walked out of Theatre, Harry spoke quietly yet clearly beside her.

'You've done a lot of work in Theatre before coming here, Kimberlie, that much I've figured out for myself.' His words were said with utter conviction. 'I just hope one day you'll trust me enough to tell me why you've lied about your qualifications.'

She sighed, knowing she had to tell him the truth. Perhaps she could get Moss to approve it. She'd have to ask Tammy, who knew far more about the business side of ASIS than Kim did. After all, she was just the medical expert on loan from the army.

Kim met his gaze, knowing she couldn't back down from him. She loved him and wanted to be as honest with him as she could. 'I really want to tell you, Harry…but I can't. Not yet.'

'What's going on, Kimberlie? There are so many questions I have, so many things that don't add up.' He raked a hand through his hair, eager for the truth.

'I know, and it's to your credit that you've realised something is…out of kilter. Just give me a few more days, Harry. Please?'

He hesitated. 'I don't like lies, Kimberlie.'

'I know.' She met his gaze.

'I presume you've heard the gossip about my marriage?'

Kim nodded.

'It was a long time ago and I'm over the pain but the fact that she lied to me, that other people have lied to me—it drives me insane. It's the one thing I cannot stand, and will not tolerate in a relationship.'

'I know and, where you and I are concerned, my feelings for you are honest. You must believe that.'

'How can I when you constantly clam up? We need to be honest with each other about *everything* and I know, so far, you haven't been.'

'You're right.'

'Then tell me,' he urged, placing his hands on her shoulders. 'Trust me, Kimberlie.'

She closed her eyes and shook her head, unable to believe the predicament she was in. 'I *do* trust you, Harry…but I can't tell you. Not right now.'

Harry looked at her for a long moment before dropping his hands and walking away. Kim closed her eyes, wanting desperately to run after him but knowing she couldn't…neither could she watch him walk away from her.

She stood there for another minute, trying desperately to get herself under control, but the numbness had settled over her and was threatening to stay. Shaking her head, she forced her legs to move and went to Recovery to check on her patient. After that, she went to A and E in search of Harry but there was no sign of him. She asked after Switch and was told he'd been discharged. Kim nodded and while things were temporarily quiet, she took the opportunity to check on not only Louanne and Cynthia but also to see how Enid had fared.

She headed to the thoracic ward and over to where Enid had been admitted. Even though it was now almost four o'clock in the morning, Enid was lying in bed, eyes wide open.

'Hi, there,' Kim said, and the other woman blinked.

'There you are, deary. I've been so worried about you.'

Kim was touched. 'Is that why you can't sleep?'

'I'm an old worry wart. What happened to the two girls on the top floor? Are they all right?'

'Cynthia's going to be fine. She was treated mainly for shock and smoke inhalation.'

'And her mother?'

'She's in ICU—ah, that stands for intensive care unit.'

'That doesn't sound too good.'

'I've just been up to check on her.' And missed Harry who'd been there just before her. 'The next twenty-four hours are critical. She was badly burned and sustained a fractured shoulder and arm as well as a few abdominal injuries.'

'Are you a surgeon?'

Kim nodded. 'Yes. We took her to Theatre straight away to stabilise her.'

'Have you been doing this work long? You look so young, dear.'

Kim smiled. 'That's funny, I feel so old. It's been a long night.'

'I'm sure it has. You go and rest.'

'Are you going to be able to sleep? I can ask the nurses to give you something.'

'I'm fine. Don't you go worrying about me. I'll have all of my family in here later today, fussing over me and telling me I should move in with them rather than be on my own.'

'Is that what you want?'

Enid sighed heavily. 'I have been thinking about it more seriously and tonight, well, it's shown me that life is unpredictable. It doesn't matter what precautions I take, I can't control what's going to happen.'

Kim nodded, thinking of how she hadn't planned to fall in love with Harry.

'I love my kids and my grandkids and, well, I've been thinking that perhaps it would be good if I got out of the city and spent more time with them. Having a family, having roots, is what counts and my daughter is already planning to build a granny flat onto the back of her house, so I'd still be living by myself but with everyone I love nice and close.'

Kim was choked with emotion. 'Sounds… perfect.' And it did. 'Looks as though you've made that decision, Enid.'

The elderly woman yawned and closed her eyes. 'Yes.'

Kim said goodbye, glad Enid would now sleep peacefully, and headed to the orthopaedic ward to find Mrs Pressman. She stopped in the doorway to the ward and watched as Harry sat beside the woman's bedside, holding her hand. Her heart turned somersaults at his tenderness and the love inside her grew.

Quietly, she walked across but wasn't surprised when he looked up. 'Should I be jealous?'

His tired smile not only warmed her heart but reassured her as well. Perhaps he'd accepted that there were just some things she couldn't tell him even though she wanted to.

He looked back at his neighbour. 'She's been through so much. Her husband died last year and then she got sick. Next she had leg ulcers and now a total hip replacement.' He shook his head.

'Does she have family close?'

'She has five sons and they're always over to see her.'

'And she has you.'

Harry nodded. 'She's always looking out for me. That's a nice feeling.'

'How did her surgery go?'

'Without complication.'

'Good.' They were both quiet for a moment before Harry kissed Mrs Pressman's hand and released it. 'Ready to go?'

'Yes.' She looked down at her theatre scrubs. 'I'll get changed and then you still owe me a decent coffee.'

'What?' They walked out of the ward and headed back towards the emergency theatre changing rooms. 'What about the coffee in the café?'

'That doesn't count. I spilt most of it.'

'True. My car's at my apartment so we can grab a cab and I can drop you off at your apartment before continuing home.'

Kim recalled she still needed to get a look into his safe and although she was dead tired, she also loved being with Harry and would take any excuse. 'My bag is with your security guard and my keys are in my bag, remember?'

He paused and looked at her. 'Well, then, I guess you'd better come back to my apartment with me.'

'I guess I'd better.' Excitement zipped through her and she had to work hard to restrain herself from grabbing him and pressing her lips to his right there and then.

'Get changed. Two minutes, Dr Mason.'

Kim was out of the changing rooms one minute and fifty-five seconds later. She'd put her earpiece back in as she didn't have any pockets in her skirt and didn't want Harry to see her holding it. She'd untied her hair so it covered both her ears, splashed a bit of water on her face to help her stay awake and focused. The sooner she could get a look inside his safe, the sooner her spying on Harry would be over. She'd get him to tell her why he'd taken the sample and that would be it. Over and done with. She had to focus on John McPhee next and she was determined to wrap things up as soon as possible so she could come clean with Harry and get on with her life.

She stopped to use the pay phone to let Tammy know she was out of Theatre and back on track.

'Who are you calling at this hour of the morning?' he asked.

'Tammy. She worries. I just leave messages on her machine so she knows I'm safe.' He seemed to accept her answer.

As though by unspoken mutual consent, they both wanted to forget about their previous conversation outside Theatres and just enjoy being with each other. Harry held her hand all the way back to his apartment and retrieved her bag from the night security guard. They rode the lift in silence and after he'd unlocked the door and gone inside, Harry gathered her close and pressed his lips to hers.

'I've been wanting to do that for hours,' he murmured against her lips before claiming them once more. Gone were the soft, sweet kisses he'd given her in the cafeteria. These were hot, hungry and extremely possessive. 'You're driving me crazy, Kimberlie. I can't sleep, I can't eat, I can barely concentrate on work.' He shook his head. 'It's nuts but I can't help it.'

'I know.' She dropped her bag to the floor and laced her fingers through his hair, bringing his mouth down on hers once more, revelling in the wild explosions that were taking place deep inside her.

Finally, they broke apart, both of them gasping for air. 'I…um…just need to go and freshen up,' she said. 'Why don't you put the coffee on?' She bent to pick up her bag, her eyes widening in alarm as she noticed it had opened when she'd dropped it and her decoder was a few inches away. Quickly, she shoved it back in and snapped it closed, praying Harry hadn't seen.

Kim looked at him as she straightened but he was standing with his eyes closed, taking deep breaths. She smiled and quickly headed to the bathroom, shutting the door. She allowed herself one small, satisfied breath before feeling behind the second mirror for the trigger to release it.

'Tammy?'

'Yeah?' her friend yawned.

'Sorry if I got you up. I'm in the bathroom.'

Pulling out the decoder, she switched on the cold tap before going to work. She opened the safe and found…a sheaf of papers. She quickly scanned them. Legal documents for the purchase of his apartment, his car, insurance—nothing out of the ordinary.

The last one was a list of names. She scanned it, recognising her own on it.

'What…?' she whispered, scanning the next page of the document.

'What is it?'

It was about the minister's death and she realised the list of names was of people Harry suspected. John McPhee's name was on the list, too, and it was underlined in red. At least *her* name wasn't underlined in red. She reported the information to Tammy.

'He's doing his own investigation. How cute.' Tammy yawned again.

'Kimberlie?'

Quickly she stuffed everything back into the safe. 'Just a second,' she called as she wiped everything down with a towel and then clicked the mirror back into place. She quickly rinsed her hands and headed back out.

'You all right?' he asked, concerned.

'Yeah. Great. Coffee ready?'

'I have iced coffee if you'd prefer.'

She smiled. 'Perhaps that might be better.'

'Better? I was going for safer!' He reached for her and she went willingly into his arms, placing her bag on the kitchen bench behind him. 'I can't seem to get enough of you.'

'Likewise.'

His lips on hers were possessive but not as hard as before. Kim sighed against him as he leant back against the bench, settling her close to his body. 'You're delicious,' he murmured as he spread tiny, hot kisses across her cheek, down around her jaw, across her neck to where her top dipped down towards her chest.

'Mmm.' Kim closed her eyes, caught up in the moment, the feeling—caught up in Harry. She tilted her head backwards to allow him greater access, feeling goose-bumps spread over her body as he trailed more kisses up her neck before gently pushing her hair back to nibble on her earlobe.

'Now you're driving *me* crazy,' she whispered. The kisses had stopped and she opened her eyes as Harry pulled back. When she looked at him, it wasn't to find him smiling, or to find him smouldering with repressed passion, as she'd hoped. Instead, his face was a mask, as though a shutter had come down, locking out all emotions.

'Harry?' She went to move back but he held her firmly in place. 'What's wrong?'

Slowly, he reached up his hand and tucked her hair behind her ear, pulling the earpiece out as he did so.

Kim gasped and tried again to move away but his arm about her waist was like a band of steel.

'What's this?'

CHAPTER NINE

'ONE of our team has swept John McPhee's office at the hospital and come up with nothing so we really need you to be at that party with Harry tomorrow.' Tammy sipped her coffee and looked at Kim. 'Kim? Earth to Kim? Are you even listening to me?'

Kim stared off into space. 'I doubt Harry will want to take me to John McPhee's or anywhere else.'

'He'll take you.'

'How can you be so sure? I mean, you heard what happened on Monday night. He *hates* me!'

'He doesn't hate you. He may feel betrayed but he doesn't hate you.'

'How can you say that?' Kim uncrossed her legs and stood to pace the floor. She shook her head. 'I still can't believe I got so carried away that he found my earpiece.'

'It's not the end of the world. At least you didn't tell him anything.'

'What was I supposed to say? "Hey, I'm glad you found that because I've been meaning to tell you I'm a spy"?'

'You're not a spy.'

'Well, I was certainly spying on him.'

'That's all over now. Moss is satisfied that Harry had nothing to do with the minister's death.'

'And what about the sample he took?'

'It's been taken care of and his motives were honest.'

'Of course they were,' Kim said hotly. 'I can't believe I spied on the man I love.'

'You weren't spying. You were checking him out.'

Kim groaned and stalked out of the room.

'I didn't mean it like that,' Tammy called.

Kim shut her bedroom door and threw herself on the bed, burying her face in the pillows. He'd just stood there, looking down at her with disdain, holding the evidence of her earpiece between his thumb and finger as though it were a tiny bomb, waiting to explode.

The whole conversation had played itself over and over in her head for the past three nights. Every time she saw him at work, the looks he gave her brought it all back once more.

'Kimberlie?' Even the way he'd said her name had shown he was repulsed by what had happened—repulsed by her. 'What's going on?'

Kim had pivoted quickly in his arms and he'd been forced to let her go. She'd snatched the earpiece out of his hand and quickly replaced it in her ear. 'Harry. Just listen.'

'To what? More of your lies?'

She'd closed her eyes, trying to think. It wouldn't matter what she said, there was no way he would believe her. Kim had opened her eyes and looked seriously at him. 'This…' she gestured to her ear '…has nothing to do with how I feel about you.'

'And what exactly is "this"? Does it have anything to do with why you're so brilliant in the operating theatre? Why you've deceived me regarding your medical qualifications?'

Kim had shaken her head and sighed, then picked up her bag and headed for the door.

'That's right. Just walk out with no explanation. That really shows me how you feel about me.'

She'd stopped with her hand on the doorhandle and slowly turned to face him, trying desperately to stop her eyes from welling with tears. 'It's not going to matter what I say, Harry. You're already judging me.' She'd deliberately tried to keep her tone level but wasn't quite sure she'd succeeded.

'So that's it?'

She'd nodded, knowing it hadn't been the time to explain. She'd desperately wanted to ignore the orders she'd been given, but she couldn't. She was a soldier and trained to follow orders. 'That's it.'

'Who do you hear through the earpiece? Can they hear us now?'

Kim sighed and shook her head, trying with all her might to hang onto the tears which had been steadily building up. She'd swallowed over the lump in her throat. 'I have to go.'

She'd opened the door and walked down the corridor, taking the stairs instead of waiting for the lift. He hadn't come after her…even though she'd desperately wanted him to.

He'd hardly spoken to her since, except when they needed to converse regarding patients. Jerry had taken over all her training and thankfully hadn't asked any questions as to why she and Harry were avoiding each other.

On one point, she at least had been given some answers. The pathology results had come in from the autopsy and had shown the cause of death had been due to propofol poisoning. Harry would have received the same results back from the sample he'd sent off to the lab so at least he would know how the minister had died. Strangely enough, the Tarparniian officials were still willing to state the minister had died of natural causes. She wasn't sure why. Perhaps announcing the truth would create more civil unrest in Tarparnii but she couldn't help thinking about what Ni Kartu had said. Japarlin would have been formally charged and had a trial in his home country had he not died. So why had John McPhee killed him? Justice was going to be served so why kill him?

ASIS now knew *who* had killed the minister and *how*, but no one was sure of *why*. It was her job to find out but she vowed to herself that the instant it was done, she would find Harry and tell him the truth. She'd confess her love, beg him to give her a second chance and then…hopefully he'd agree and they could live happily ever after.

Oh, please, she prayed, squeezing her eyes as tightly shut as she could, her hands clenched desperately into fists.

'Kim?' Tammy knocked on her door, waited a second and then came into the room. 'You need to get past this, honey.' Tammy lay down next to her. 'What do you say we head downtown and go see Crazy Shadows? I saw Switch last night and he showed me his sutures.' Tammy sighed dramatically and clutched her hand to her chest.

Kim laughed through her tears and socked Tammy one with a pillow. 'You're crazy.'

'It'll be fun.'

'Oh, yeah, watching you and Switch making eyes at each other all night long. What a thrill. That's *just* what I need—not.'

'You might have a point there.' Tammy raised herself up on her elbow. 'This is the real thing with Harry?'

Kim nodded sadly. 'No other for me.'

'Really? He's it?'

'He's the man I love now and for ever more… and he hates my guts.'

'No, he doesn't. He's just confused because he has no answers. We'll wrap this job up and then you and Harry can live happily ever after.'

'And what about ASIS? What about the army?'

'What about them?' Tammy's question was serious. 'Come on, Kim. What about them?'

'I don't know,' she wailed. 'I…I love my job. I love being in the army, I love travelling but now…now… The other night, the night of the fire, one of the ladies who lived on the second floor said her family had been bothering her to move out of her apartment and live with them. I think she initially took it as a sign that they were trying to take away her independence but she said the fire made her realise all they wanted was for her to be near them.'

'You want to be near Harry. That's natural because you love him.'

'But what about my job? I love my job.'

'More than Harry?'

'No. That's the point, though. Do I throw everything away for Harry? Sacrifice myself on the altar of love?'

'Will you actually be *throwing* it away? I mean, you can still be a doctor, just not in the army.'

'I'd be changing for him.'

'Would you? Or would you be changing for you? Either way, the question you need to ask yourself is—is he worth it?'

Kim spent most of Friday trying to catch up with Harry. She was in Theatre from two in the morning until two in the afternoon and then had clinic to get through. After that, she did a quick ward round.

She stopped by to see Louanne, who'd been transferred to the burns unit, and was pleased to see Cynthia sitting beside her mother's bed, reading from the latest glossy magazine.

'Anything interesting going on in the world of fashion?' Kim asked as she read Louanne's chart, pleased with her progress.

'Nothing new.' Cynthia added, 'It helps relax Mum if I read out loud and then she usually drifts off to sleep, like she's done now.'

Kim smiled and pulled over another chair. 'How are things going with you?'

'Oh…you know.'

'Where are you staying?'

'With a lady called Enid. She lives on the second floor of my building and she's really sweet. In fact, all the neighbours have been really sweet. Enid's getting ready to go live with her family but she said she'll stay there for as long as Mum and I need her help.'

'She's a lovely lady.'

'Yeah…and, also, the fire department have said that our apartment isn't a total wipe-out because if it was, they might have had to tear down the whole building and then everyone would have been out of their homes. It would have been so unfair but it's brill that didn't happen.'

'Brill.' Kim nodded. 'Has the insurance company contacted you?'

'Yeah. Man, I tell you, those guys are scary.'

'Do you need any help sorting things out?'

'Nah. Jamie, he's a guy who lives on the second floor, he does that kind of thing for a living…well, he's training at uni, so he's been brill.'

Kim smiled at the way Cynthia's eyes glazed over with delight as she said Jamie's name. 'I'm sure he is.' She glanced up at the clock. 'Listen, I have to run but I'll be around tomorrow so I'll see you then. Oh, and say hi to your mum for me.'

'I will. She'll be sorry she missed you. She enjoys your daily visits.'

'So do I.'

Kim bolted to Harry's office only to have his secretary say that he was in a meeting.

Was he really in a meeting or was he just saying that to avoid her?

His secretary was in the process of locking everything up for the weekend and Kim waited until she'd gone before she went back to Harry's office and tried the doorhandle. Sure enough, it was locked, but that didn't mean he wasn't in there.

Digging into her trousers, she pulled out the tiny tools she needed and quickly picked his lock. She opened the door and discovered he wasn't in his office. She frowned. Perhaps his secretary had told the truth. Perhaps he really was at a meeting.

'Kimberlie?'

She jumped in fright, banging her shoulder against the open door as she stumbled further into his office. He merely walked straight past her and dumped an armload of files onto his desk.

'What do you want?' He was brisk and to the point…and she loved everything about him. Her gaze hungrily devoured him, glad of the opportunity to be alone with him for the first time in some days. He gestured to the miniature tools in her hand. 'I see you had no difficulty getting into my office.'

Kim quickly put her hand in her pocket and came further into the room. He raised his eyebrows, indicating he was waiting for her to speak.

'Uh…I just wondered whether you still wanted me to accompany you to John McPhee's tonight?'

He was silent for so long Kim wondered whether she'd spoken the question out loud or merely thought it.

'John and his wife are expecting both of us.'

'OK. Good. Um…do you want me to meet you at your apartment?'

'Eight o'clock. Now, if you'll excuse me…' He gestured to the pile of papers in front of him.

'Oh, yeah. Of course.' She stumbled backwards. 'Well, I'll see you later tonight, then.' She closed his door behind her, wondering if she should lock him in but deciding against it. At least he was still willing to take her to John McPhee's party…which, when she thought about it, was completely strange. She'd honestly thought he wouldn't want anything to do with her but here he was, willing to accompany her. Just as Tammy had said he would.

She headed out of the hospital, thinking about things as she walked to her apartment. Harry was quite willing to go along with the situation, to find her in his office with tools in her hands. She shook her head, unable to believe she'd once again been sloppy. She was *never* sloppy…well, she hadn't been until she'd been distracted by Harry throughout this entire mission.

He seemed to be accepting things and that alone caused more concern than anything else. Had Moss already brought him into ASIS? Tammy had said the information regarding the sample had been taken care of and that Moss was satisfied with what Harry had done. She was a person who followed her instincts and right now they were telling her that Harry had been approached by ASIS. How much he'd been told was the unclear part. She shook her head. She hadn't wanted him brought into this life, especially as she had decided she would willingly give it all up for him.

First, though, she had to finish this mission before she could sit down with Harry and tell him everything. Tell him that she wouldn't be keeping anything from him in the future, no lies, no secrets. Nothing would ever come between them again…if only he'd give her a second chance.

When she arrived home, it was to find Tammy waiting for her. 'Going to the ball, Cinderella?'

'Yes.' Her tone was noncommittal.

'Well, don't sound so happy about it.'

'Has Moss spoken to Harry?'

Tammy didn't break eye contact but Kim noticed a change in her expression.

'Oh, let me guess, you can't talk about it.'

'No. I can't.'

'I'll take that as a yes, then.' Kim ground her teeth together in frustration and slammed her fist into the sofa. 'Why did he bring him in? I suppose he wants Harry to help him with reconnaissance in Tarparnii and the other countries Harry already visits. Moss doesn't give a hoot about anyone's life—only about ASIS and how he can manipulate people to get them to do what he wants.'

Tammy only shrugged at her words before saying quietly, 'Come on. You don't have much time to shower and change before you need to meet Harry. I've taken the liberty of choosing your outfit.'

'I suppose it has all the usual trimmings, like safe decoders, dusting power, laser weapons and a grenade launcher.'

Tammy laughed. 'So nice to see you have your sense of humour back. Into the shower.'

The distance they had to travel wasn't all that far but the silence in the car was unbearable.

'Thank you for driving me. I could have taken a taxi.' Kim glanced across at him as they stopped at a red light. His jaw was clenched firmly and she wondered if he was going to talk to her at all tonight. Not that she could completely blame him. If he'd lied and deceived her, she would have found it hard to forgive. Still…it would be nice to have a *little* bit of conversation.

Harry didn't say a word until they pulled up in John's street, which was lined with cars. He switched off the engine, undid his seat belt and climbed from the car. Kim quickly got out, not expecting him to come around and hold her door.

'Let's get this over with,' he murmured, and headed off. Kim managed to keep stride with him, and when they reached the front door he rang the doorbell.

'At least *try* to look as though you're happy, Harry.'

He stared at her for a long moment, making her feel extremely self-conscious. She tugged at the bottom of her navy silk top which matched her silk pants. The outfit was one of her favourites mainly because the pants had several slim-lined pockets in them, easy to carry the few tools she needed when on missions.

She gazed up into Harry's eyes but found nothing there reminiscent of the man she'd fallen in love with. His blue eyes were shuttered and cold, freezing out anyone who dared to venture too close to him. The door opened and he quickly looked away, forcing a smile as their hostess beckoned them in.

'Hello. I'm Kat. Welcome.'

Kim forced herself not to stare at the woman as they stepped over the threshold into John McPhee's very comfortable home. Kat McPhee—her name had been down on John's dossier as his spouse. The agency hadn't been able to get much information on Kat's background but what little they did have said she was a citizen of New Zealand.

Kim cleared her throat. 'Kat? That's a lovely name. Is it short for anything?'

'Kateka.'

Kim smiled. 'Very pretty.' She followed Kat into the house. 'Is it a family name?'

'Yes, as a matter of fact it is. My great-grandmother's name was Kateka. It means "one who delivers".'

'And that's a Maori name, isn't it?' Harry asked, and Kim could have kissed him right there on the spot for chiming in.

'No. Tarparniian.' Kat waved to John who was on the other side of the room and soon the anaesthetist was making his way over.

'Harry. Kim. Good to see you.' He shook hands with them both and offered them a drink, gesturing to the bar with his wineglass, sloshing red wine onto the floor.

'I'm so glad we didn't end up getting carpeting in here, but if I don't clean that up now, it's going to stain the floorboards,' Kat scolded her husband, and excused herself.

'Never mind her. Come on over to the bar,' John said. 'What'll it be?'

'Champagne?' Kim asked.

'We have plenty of that tonight. Plenty.'

'Harry never did mention what the party was in honour of. Is it someone's birthday?'

'No. Just a celebration for the sake of having a celebration.' John tapped the side of his nose.

'Know what I mean?' He laughed and swayed a little. Harry grabbed his arm.

'Whoa. Steady on, there.' Harry smiled. 'I'll get the champagne.'

'While you do,' Kim added, 'would you mind telling me where I can find the bathroom?'

'Uh… Oh, yeah. Down the hall and to the right, third door on the left. No, fourth door. Oh, never mind. You'll find it,' John slurred, and propped himself up on the wooden bar.

Kim found the bathroom, and also the room which was John's study. She glanced around and slipped in, taking a casual look around the room. 'Did you get the information on John's wife?' she asked Tammy through her earpiece.

'Yes. We're checking it out. Don't make a move just yet. We need at least an hour.'

Kim made her way out of the study and back to the party, smiling brightly at Harry and wondering why he was giving her a quizzical look. 'Thank you,' she said, taking the glass of champagne from him. When she was in this type of situation, she found it easier to order one drink of alcohol at the beginning of the night and use the glass to nurse her way through the evening, barely drinking a drop.

An hour later, the party was in full swing with people spread out all over the house. Harry had started to relax and at one point had even put his arm around her shoulders. Kim had leaned against him, relishing the feel of his body against hers. There was a mixed group of people here but the majority were from the hospital and it was interesting to see everyone's reaction to the news that Harry and Kim had come together.

'But you hardly know each other,' one of the nurses said.

Kim had felt Harry tense beside her so she laughed. 'Things happen quickly with me.' She turned and smiled up at him. 'We may not have known each other long but we know each other deeply.'

Harry's gaze had held hers and she hoped she was conveying her message. What she'd said was true. She felt as though she'd known him for most of her life and that she'd been searching for him for ever. All she wanted was for him to place his lips on hers, to reassure her that she hadn't completely destroyed the feelings he'd previously felt for her. But he didn't. Instead, he looked down at the floor before making an excuse to go and get another drink.

'That's so sweet.' The nurse grinned. 'I hadn't heard anything about the two of you on the hospital grapevine. How did you manage to keep it under the radar?'

'Kim?' It was Tammy's voice through her ear-piece.

Kim smiled at the nurse. 'I actually have no idea. I'd better go give him a hand with the drinks. Excuse me.' She made her way through the crowd of people. 'Tam?'

'We've got the info. Kateka McPhee, nee Zefari. Has been a member of a Tarparniian right-wing radical group since she was a teen-ager. Our Tarparniian expert says she's been wanted for questioning regarding a few other in-cidents over ten years ago but they haven't been able to locate her—until now. A warrant for her arrest is being processed and we're sending the local police around with it. They should be there in fifteen to twenty minutes. If you can get us some evidence that she was involved with Japarlin's death, there'll finally be something solid on her.'

'I'll take a look.' Kim glanced across the room to the bar. Harry was standing there, leaning against the solid wood, watching every move she made. She smiled and pointed in the direction of the bathroom. He nodded and turned away to talk to John who was gladly refilling his own glass along with everyone else's.

Kim almost jumped for joy when she discov-ered a queue outside the door, of people waiting to use the convenience. She headed back down the corridor as though she was just drifting, glancing at the pictures on the wall.

Checking no one was watching, she went into the study and began going through the drawers in John's desk. She checked the files on top and then, after checking the line was still there for the bathroom, she unlocked the filing cabinet—pleased to have found the key in John's top drawer.

'Nothing.'

'OK. You've done all the obvious places. Try the not so obvious.'

Kim checked behind the pictures on the wall but there was no safe to be found. She was just heading out when a wooden board creaked beneath her foot. She glanced down and returned to John's desk, looking at the floor.

'Hang on.' She bent down on all fours and crawled beneath the desk, tapping the floor lightly with her knuckles. Hollow…hollow… solid. She smiled. 'I think we have a winner.' Kim reached out and grabbed the letter opener off the desk and levered up the floorboard.

'Papers. Lots of papers.' She unfolded a few. 'Faxes with directions, Japarlin's travel itinerary.'

'Excellent. Get some happy snaps.'

Kim pulled a small digital camera out her pocket and did as she was told. 'Do you want me to bring the papers in?'

'No. Leave them there for the local police to find. We'll tell them where to look.'

'OK.' She returned the papers to their hiding place and as she crawled out from beneath the desk, she slipped the camera back into her pocket.

'What are you doing in here!' Kat's eyes were flashing wildly as she stood in the doorway, glaring at Kim. 'You're not supposed to be in here.'

Kim smiled, putting her hand onto the desk in order to slip the letter opener back where it belonged. 'You startled me.' She put her other hand to her ear and pretended to be putting her earring back on. 'Sorry. I was waiting for the toilet and there was a line and I wandered in here and found a very interesting article lying open on your husband's desk.' She pointed to the open journal. 'I sat down to read it and started fiddling with my earring.' She shrugged, a little embarrassed. 'Anyway, it fell off and I had to crawl down here to get it. I'm sorry. I know I shouldn't have come in here but it's such a nice room.'

She rolled her eyes and headed over to the door. 'I'm only a service registrar so all I can afford is a two-bedroom apartment, which I share with one of my friends. I would give *anything* to have a study like this, especially when I do so much studying.' She laughed nervously again, hoping she wasn't overdoing things. She pointed to the hallway. 'I'll just go see if the line has dwindled.' She headed out of the room, concerned when Kat didn't follow her.

'I think she's checking on me,' Kim said, continuing her way straight through the house towards the front door. 'How much longer until the cops arrive?'

'Kimberlie?' Harry caught up with her. 'What's going on?'

'Can we go now, Harry? Please?' Her tone was urgent and she desperately needed him to do what she'd asked. Instead, he stood looking down at her, confusion written all over his face.

She glanced over his shoulder and saw Kat come out of the study. Quickly, Kim grabbed Harry's shirt and tugged him closer as she edged backwards. Soon her back was against the wall and she laced her fingers around his neck, almost pressuring his head down so their lips could meet.

'Kiss me,' she whispered. 'Now!'

Thankfully, he did as she said and clamped his mouth firmly over hers. Everything flew from her head as she tasted him hungrily. He placed his hands on the wall on either side of her head and leaned his body against the length of hers. Kim groaned with desire, loving the way they felt together. She'd thought this might never happen again, to feel his body so close to hers, to have his scent winding itself around her and drugging her senses.

It didn't matter that his kiss was punishing. She didn't mind and, in fact, she relished the pressure, the hot and hard emotions that were surging through her. It was as though he was putting all his frustrations into the kiss—and she met him head on. The past few days had been unbearable, being so close to him yet so far away.

Breathing heavily, he broke off and stared down at her, his eyes glazed with a mixture of anger and desire. He'd never been more irresistible.

'Kimberlie!' he growled. 'Don't do this to me.'

She saw the pain and desolation in his gaze and realised, perhaps for the first time, just how much she'd hurt him.

'Harry… I…' Unable to control her feelings, Kim felt tears well in her eyes. How could she have hurt him? She loved him! 'I…' She stopped again, desperately wanting to tell him everything but knowing she couldn't—not yet. She was so close. The end was so near. If only he would wait just a few more hours. That was all it should take to wrap this investigation up and then they could sort out their relationship.

Harry shifted away and shook his head. 'Still can't tell me what's going on, eh?'

'It's not that I don't want to. Harry, I *do*,' she said imploringly, but he shook his head and raked his hand through his hair in a gesture of frustration she'd come to recognise and love. Her heart broke a little bit more as he glanced at her with a look of contempt on his face.

'There you are.' Kat came up to her, ignoring Harry. 'Come with me.' Kat grabbed Kim's arm and started dragging her away. The other woman's grip was fierce and Kim blindly followed, her gaze holding Harry's as she went.

'Kim?' Tammy's voice came through her earpiece and Kim snapped her head around to look at the back of Kat's black-haired head and back to reality. 'What's going on?'

'Get your hands off me.' Kim wrenched her arm back and stalked past Kat, out onto the front lawn.

'Get out of there, a.s.a.p.,' Tammy said.

'Not so fast.' Kat grabbed Kim's shoulder and spun her around. 'What were you doing in my husband's study?'

'I told you. I sat down, read an article in the journal and dropped my earring. I bent down to pick it up and you walked in.'

Harry had followed the two women outside and was watching them. There were several other people outside, enjoying the warm evening air, who had stopped their conversations to listen. Harry edged closer, not sure what was going on but not liking Kat's open hostility towards Kim.

'No. You were looking at the papers, weren't you?' Kat's brown eyes flashed with pure hatred. 'Who are you? What agency do you work for?'

'What?' Kim looked at the other woman with incredulity.

Kat slapped her across the face and Kim was astounded. Her hand automatically came up to touch her cheek, which was burning with pain.

'Hey.' Harry stepped forward immediately, placing himself between the two women. 'What's going on?'

'As if you didn't know. I can't believe you volunteered to operate on that *p'tak*.' With a loud grunt, Kat landed a kick fair and square in Harry's chest, sending him backwards into Kim.

'Ugh.' She fell to the ground with Harry sprawled half on top of her. 'Harry? Harry? Are you OK?'

He moaned and sucked in a breath. Kim could feel her blood beginning to boil and shifted out from beneath him. How dared Kat hit the man she loved?

Kat was speaking rapidly in Tarparniian. Kim's knowledge of the language was fairly thin but just from the woman's facial expressions and the inflection in her tone she got the gist of what was being said.

She stood and stepped away from Harry, giving herself room to move if necessary. 'What did you do that for?'

'He's one of *them.*' Kat spat in his direction. 'So are you.' With that, Kat lunged towards Kim, meaning to strike her once more. Kim deftly blocked her, realising the woman was well trained. She ducked before landing a kick to Kat's stomach.

Harry was stunned as he watched the two women. Arms and legs were everywhere, both of them taking as many hits as they received. 'Kimberlie.' He whispered her name, unable to believe what he was seeing.

Kat's hard, flat palm connected with Kimberlie's head and she grunted with pain.

Harry grimaced, not quite sure what to do. He continued to watch as Kimberlie kicked Kat once in the chest with one foot and then elbowed her in the back of the head as she doubled over. His eyes widened as he recognised the move. 'You're the one who attacked me!'

He looked away, unable to believe he'd been played for a complete fool. When he'd found out what his wife had been up to, the sense of disgust, betrayal and humiliation had been overwhelming. Now, as he recognised his true feelings for Kimberlie—that he loved her, more deeply, more passionately than he'd love any other woman—the feelings he'd experienced years ago seemed shallow in comparison.

Harry couldn't bring himself to look at her and slowly got to his feet. His chest was sore as he tried to breathe and he wasn't sure whether it was from Kat's kick or Kimberlie's betrayal.

It was then he saw John coming out of the house, dropping his glass of red wine in shock at seeing his wife fighting on the front lawn. The look slowly changed to one of determination and Harry watched as John walked over to a garden statue and picked it up, heading in Kimberlie's direction.

The two women were still fighting hard. Kimberlie's hair had come loose from her band.

Red curls bounced around as she jumped onto one foot and kicked with the other, landing a blow to Kat's shoulder. She spun around quickly, her hair flicking her in the face, and landed another blow to the side of Kat's head with her foot.

Kat went down. Kimberlie stood there, gasping for breath. John was coming up behind her, the statue firmly in his hands. Harry didn't have time to call out. Kim was totally focused on Kat and he knew she'd have no time to react to John's surprise attack.

Harry did the only thing he could do. He launched himself at John. The anaesthetist came crashing to the ground as Harry tackled him, the statue smashing.

'Harry. Get off,' John yelled. 'You don't know what you're doing.' John brought his elbow up, whacking Harry across the face before twisting out to stand up. Harry recoiled but recovered quickly enough to get to his feet in time to fend off the blows John was trying to inflict upon him.

'Harry!' He heard Kimberlie's cry of anguish but ignored it. His fist connected to one side of John's face. His other fist sank into John's stomach.

'I know what you did,' he said between clenched teeth. He landed another blow to the anaesthetist, amazed at the adrenaline and anger coursing through him. 'Cold-blooded murder.' He hit John once more and the anaesthetist fell to the ground, his lip bleeding, his face bruised. He didn't move.

Harry raised his fist.

'No.'

Kimberlie's voice cut through his thoughts and he turned, fist still ready.

'It's over.' As she spoke, Harry saw Kat move. He glared down, unable to speak in time to warn Kimberlie. In the next instant Kat, who was still lying on the ground, swung her leg around, literally knocking Kimberlie off her feet.

She came crashing down, landing flat on her back, and moaned in pain. Harry glanced back at John but he was out. Police sirens were drawing closer and some of the people watching on the front lawn started to disperse. Kimberlie was lying on the ground, her face cut and bruised, her clothes ripped in places and stained, her hair in a wild mess.

Kat was getting to her feet again.

'Kimberlie!' This time he was able to get the word out and she quickly looked to where the other woman was.

With astounding agility Kim pushed up with her hands and flipped to her feet. Harry's eyes widened. Who *was* this woman he'd fallen in love with? He swallowed, unable to tear his gaze away and unable to move. The successful blows John had managed to get in were starting to pound and Harry realised it had been a long time since he'd taken a beating and then it had been on the rugby field.

Kat struck Kim a few times and he heard her grunt in pain. She fought on. He could see the determination in her face. There was no way she was going to let Kat win. With one almighty kick Kim knocked Kat down onto the grass…for good this time.

Kim buckled to her knees when the other woman didn't move. Was it over? Was Kat faking again? Was she catching her breath? Getting ready for another onslaught?

The police were pulling up, blue and red flashing lights surrounding the area.

Kim crawled over and checked Kat's pulse and then her eyes, before collapsing next to her.

'Tammy—she's down.'

'Do you still have the camera?'

Kim forced her hand to work and felt her pants pocket. 'Yes.'

'Who are you talking to?' Harry demanded, as he checked that John was still breathing.

Kim closed her eyes. She couldn't deal with Harry now. She was totally exhausted and sore and her ankle hurt so much she wanted to cry.

'Tammy.'

'The earpiece?'

Kimberlie didn't answer. Harry knelt down and checked Kat's pulse and pupils, wishing he had a medical torch. He ran his hands over the woman's arms and legs, feeling the bones. 'Her left radius feels fractured.'

'She fell on it,' Kim muttered.

'She'll need X-rays.' He paused. 'Who is she?'

'Kateka Zefari. Wanted in Tarparnii. That's all I know.' Kim tried to sit up and winced when she moved her ankle. Sitting forward, she tried to examine it but her shoulder and arm started aching every time she moved them. She moaned in pain.

'What's wrong?'

'My ankle.'

'You were standing on it just fine from what I could see.'

'Adrenaline.' Kim shrugged.

'Agent Mason?' The officer addressed both of them, unsure who was who.

'Yes?' Kim answered wearily, then waved in Kat's direction. 'She's all yours.'

'And her husband?'

'Over there.' Harry pointed to where John was still unconscious on the ground. '*Agent* Mason?'

Kim rolled her eyes and sighed dejectedly. 'Dr Mason. Agent Mason. Major Mason. Take your pick, Harry.' She was exhausted and just wanted to sleep. She collapsed back onto the ground and closed her eyes, trying not to concentrate on the pain.

'Is there an ambulance coming?'

Why were Harry's words so sluggish?

'It's on it's way, sir,' the officer replied. His words were sluggish, too. Why? They weren't the ones who'd just fought the most crazy fight they'd ever experienced. She was.

'I want to speak to the paramedics when they arrive.'

'Yes, sir.'

'Kimberlie?' Harry knelt beside her. When he received no response, he tapped her face. 'Kimberlie?'

She moaned and winced, her eyes clenched tight. Harry checked her pulse before running his hands over her arms and legs. When he reached her ankle, she yelled in pain.

He carefully checked her ankle. She needed medical treatment. 'Kimberlie?' He received no reply. He shook his head, unsure what to do next.

He brushed the hair out of her face, looking down at the woman he loved—but didn't know.

Harry gently touched her ear and found the earpiece. He took it out and put it in his own ear.

'Hello? Tammy?'

'Harry! What's going on?'

'Kimberlie requires medical attention on her right ankle. Do you want her taken to Sydney General or somewhere else? One of your medical experts needs to take a look at her.'

'She *is* our medical expert,' Tammy said, and Harry heard the worry in her voice.

'I'll take her to Sydney General, then.'

'OK. I'll come and get the camera.'

'Camera?'

'Don't ask too many questions, Harry.'

'Right.' There was bitterness in his tone. 'I forgot. No questions, no answers.'

'Sorry.'

Harry looked down at Kimberlie as he spoke. 'So am I.'

'And this time she's awake,' Jerry said as he came into the A and E cubicle where Kim was lying on the bed. 'Last time I looked in on you, you were still…sleeping.'

Kim tried to smile but ended up wincing instead. 'I feel like I've been hit by a very large truck.'

Jerry laughed. 'You look like it, too.' He picked up her chart and read it. 'Any pain?'

'I'm good.'

'Don't be a heroine, Kim. If you need analgesics, ask for them.'

She nodded slowly. Jerry pulled back the blankets and took a good look at her ankle. 'You've done a good job on this.' He grabbed the X-rays and took one out to show her. 'Thankfully, you didn't fracture anything, even though you gave it a pretty good try.'

Kim sighed. 'Good.'

'Do you remember much from when you were brought in?'

'No.' She vaguely remembered Harry's voice barking out orders left, right and centre, but since then she hadn't heard or seen him.

'I must say, you've all created quite a stir. You, John and his wife.'

'How are they?'

'John had a fractured jaw and his missus has a fractured arm and a few broken ribs. You, on the other hand, seem to be made of rubber. Just your ankle and that's it.'

'I guess she didn't get as many hits in as I thought.'

Jerry shook his head. 'Still hard to believe you were fighting. The buzz on the grapevine is that you're some type of secret agent.'

Kim nodded. 'Can always count on the grapevine.'

'Is it true?'

Kim met and held Jerry's gaze. 'If I told you, I'd have to kill you.'

Jerry's smile was slow. 'I'll take that as a yes,' he whispered.

The curtain to the cubicle was wrenched back and Harry walked in. The butterflies, which had been taking a well-earned rest inside Kim's stomach, suddenly burst to life. Her heart rate increased and her lips parted to allow the shallow breaths room to escape.

She looked at him, not breaking eye contact, willing him to speak. To say something. Anything!

'It's beginning to feel a little crowded in here,' Jerry mumbled. 'I'll come back later, Kim.'

After he'd gone, she and Harry continued to stare at each other until Kim could stand it no more.

'Say something,' she whispered. He didn't. He simply stood beside her bed, arms folded defensively across his chest, his gaze piercing hers. It was as though he could see right into her soul and she felt so exposed—but that was good, she reminded herself. It was good that Harry could see the real her at last. Pity she had to be so beaten up and probably looking the worst she'd ever looked in the time they'd known each other but at least the truth was out. Now…now all she had to do was find the courage to take the next step and try healing the rift between them. It wasn't going to be easy.

'Harry, you have questions, I know.'

'Going to answer them now?'

'Are John and Kat in custody?'

'Yes.'

She gasped. 'The camera!' She was currently wearing a hospital gown.

'Tammy has it.'

She relaxed. 'So you know that much at least.'

'How long have you been working for ASIS?'

'Five years.'

'You said your fiancé died four years ago. Was that on a mission? Was he with ASIS, too?'

'Yes. Chris directly disobeyed my orders and went back into that fire.'

Harry nodded, thinking back to the conversation they'd had in the cafeteria and remembered she'd made a slip about Chris and disobeying orders. What other slips had she made that he'd been too stupid, too love-struck to pick up on?

'Has anything you've said to me been true?'

'Of course,' she implored. 'Harry, you have to believe me—'

'Believe you? Oh, that's rich.' He raked a hand through his hair. His voice was low but she could hear the pain. 'You've constantly lied to me, Kimberlie.' He broke off and shook his head. 'You thought I was involved with Japarlin's death.'

'That was my job. My mission, Harry. I was sent here to investigate.'

'But you were here *before* the death occurred.'

'Only because ASIS had been tipped off. They'd been told an attempt might be made on his life. Security was stepped up to protect him while he was recovering post-op, only he never made it that far. I'd been given a list of people who were connected with Tarparnii and you were on that list. I'd been told to make sure I was in that operating theatre.'

'So you gave Edington a reason to switch with you.'

'Yes. Everything was going according to plan, Harry…that is, until I met you.'

He clenched his jaw. 'So you thought you'd bump me to the top of the list, eh? Do a *thorough* investigation on me.'

'No! That's not what I meant.'

'That's how it felt, Kimberlie. I don't know anything any more. I don't even know if Kimberlie Mason is your real name.'

'It is. You know me better than you think, Harry. Honestly.'

'*Honestly?* Do you even know the meaning of the word? You were *investigating* me, Kimberlie.'

'Yes, and you were investigating me.'

'What?' Harry frowned for a moment before shaking his head. 'You've been through my safe.' He shook his head in disbelief.

'I was ordered to.'

'And that's all you do, is it? Blindly follow orders?'

'Harry, you don't understand.'

'You've got that right.' He looked away, grinding his teeth together before meeting her gaze once more. 'Did any of our time together mean anything to you?'

'*Yes.*' How could she make him realise the truth? 'It meant *everything* to me.'

'You have a funny way of showing it.' His words were said with disdain and she could feel tears beginning to choke her throat.

'It was my job.'

'Well, let me say you're very good at it. Was seducing me part of the plan?'

'No!' She was appalled that he thought that. 'Harry, I *love* you.'

He snorted with derision. 'Love? How can you possibly know what the word means? How can you claim to love someone when you can't even be honest with them?' he asked rhetorically.

She tried to wipe her eyes but ended up wincing with pain. She hated feeling so weak, so handicapped, especially when she needed to be at her strongest to make him see how perfect they were together. 'Every moment we shared together was special. It was real, *very* real, and I tried so hard not to fall in love with you, but I did and I don't regret it for one instant.'

'Shared together? That's sweet. Shared together—with Tammy and goodness knows who else listening in.'

Kim swallowed, unable to refute his words. 'Harry, I—'

'No. Don't bother, Kimberlie.'

'Harry,' she implored, but he started to walk away. 'Harry? *Please*, don't walk away.'

He turned and looked at her…and it was the look of a stranger.

'I don't know who you are, Kimberlie, and I'm not sure I *want* to know any more.' With that, he walked out of her life and she was powerless to stop him.

CHAPTER TEN

'KIMMY?' Her mother knocked on her bedroom door. 'Kimmy, darling. Tammy's on the phone.'

Kim dried her eyes and blew her nose. 'Come in,' she called. Her mother came in with the portable phone.

'Aw, darling.' She sat on the bed and hugged her daughter. 'It'll work itself out.' Kim found it hard to hold back the tears when her mother held her. Eileen put the phone to her ear. 'Tammy? She'll call you back later. What? OK, dear. Bye.' Eileen disconnected the call and put the phone down on the bed. 'Tammy said she has to go out but she'll ring you later tonight.'

Kim pulled back to look at her mother. 'I need a tissue.' Eileen held out the box and, taking a tissue, Kim blew her nose again. 'Tam's a good friend.'

'Yes, she is. She cares about you, just like your father and I do.'

Kim nodded.

'And who else?' her mother asked.

'Sorry?'

'Who else cares about you?'

'What do you mean, Mum?'

'What's his name, Kimmy?' Eileen smiled. 'I doubt it's your sore ankle that's made you this upset. Only a man—a man you obviously love—could make you sob so heartily. I've left you alone, hoping you'd work things out, but now I've come to the conclusion you need to talk, so…out with it, missy.'

'Oh, Mum, I've made a big mess of everything.' A fresh bout of tears threatened to overwhelm her.

'We can fix it.'

'I don't think so. Harry doesn't want anything to do with me and I don't blame him.'

Eileen straightened. 'Well, that's just ridiculous. You're one of the most generous, kind-hearted and special people I've ever met.'

Kim smiled, her skin tight. 'You're a little biased there, Mum.'

'Absolutely. If this Harry doesn't realise what a fool he's been, regardless of what happened between you, perhaps he's not good enough for you.'

'Oh, but he is,' she said desolately. 'He's just perfect for me.'

'Then what's the problem?'

Kim took a deep breath. 'I...well...I lied to him. I had to,' she rushed on quickly. 'So I don't blame him if he never wants to see me again.'

'Why did you lie? Was it necessary?'

'Yes. Oh, yes. I didn't want him to get hurt.'

'There you are, then. There was a good motive behind the deception.' Eileen hugged her daughter once more. 'If Harry knows you well enough, I'm sure he'll come to his senses. So...' Eileen grinned like a schoolgirl, her eyes bright with excitement. 'Tell me more about him. Is he handsome?'

Kim giggled, then sighed romantically. 'He's gorgeous.' She launched into a description of Harry. It felt wonderful to be able to talk about the way he made her feel. Her mother was right. Talking about him helped and she now felt as though a ray of hope had opened up through the dark clouds that had followed her around the past few weeks.

Her father called them to lunch and, after devouring a sandwich, she decided to go out. 'I think I need some fresh air.'

'Where are you headed?' her father asked.

'Black Mountain. Thought I might go to the Botanic Gardens.'

'Will you be all right to drive with your ankle? I don't want you to hurt it when it's just starting to get better,' her father said.

'I should be all right.'

'How about I drive you?'

Kim smiled, amazed at how a little fussing and a lot of love from her parents helped her feel more in control of her out-of-control life.

'Thanks, Dad. I'd appreciate it. At least I don't need my crutches any more.'

'At least you didn't break it!' Eileen shook her head. 'All that gallivanting you do in the army. I'm surprised you haven't been hurt before now.'

'Mum, we've been over this.'

'I know.' Eileen held up her hands in defence. 'I'm sorry. I know you like the travel and the excitement, but you've been doing it for years now, Kimmy, and you can't spend the rest of your life gallivanting around the world with no commitments.'

Kim had heard this speech before and knew that if her parents had any idea of what she *really* did, they'd be even more worried than usual. This time, though, her mother's words made sense and she realised it was because she'd been feeling discontented with her life ever since she'd met Harry.

Harry—it all came back to Harry.

'You ready to go now, Kimmy?' her father asked as he picked up his car keys.

'Yes.'

'Go and relax,' Eileen said. 'You've always loved the gardens.'

Kim smiled. 'Yes, Mum,' she said, and hugged her mother close. 'Thanks for always being there for me,' she whispered in her ear. 'You're the greatest.'

'Oh, get away with you,' Eileen said, and when Kim looked at her mother, it was to see her eyes shining with tears. Kim smiled and turned away.

'Ready, Dad.'

'And take your phone,' her mother said as they headed out the door. 'You can call us when you're ready to be picked up.'

A few hours later, Kim felt much better. She was beneath a shady tree, lying on her back, watching the clouds, enjoying the texture of the grass. 'I do love this place,' she whispered, and sighed, making imaginary pictures out of the clouds.

When her phone buzzed, she sat up and pulled it from her pocket. The caller ID said it was her mother.

'Almost ready to come home?'

'What's the time?' Kim checked her watch. 'Wow. That late.'

'You're obviously relaxing.'

'Yes. I'm in my favourite spot on the eucalypt lawn, lying on the grass beneath a eucalyptus tree, watching the clouds.' She smiled. 'It's like a little slice of heaven.'

'I'm sorry I disturbed you.' Her mother laughed. 'Ready to be picked up?'

'Yes.'

'You can stay longer if you like.'

'No. I can always come back tomorrow. See you soon.' Kim disconnected the call and lay down again, looking back up at the clouds. After a moment she closed her eyes, surprised at how tired she was feeling. The past month had been one huge roller-coaster and she was drained—both mentally and physically.

It had taken her less than two weeks to fall in love with Harry and now the past two weeks without him had seemed meaningless.

In the operation debrief, when she'd been told the McPhees had been contracted by members of the Tarparnii government to eliminate Mr Japarlin, Kim had only thought about Harry.

When Moss had bawled her out for being so careless in breaking her cover when she'd fought Kateka Zefari in front of a crowd, Kim hadn't cared. Now that people knew she was an ASIS agent, her use to them had become limited. Her services were no longer required at Sydney General and she'd been put on sick leave, effective immediately.

Tammy's theory had been interesting. She'd suggested Kim had subconsciously wanted to blow her cover so that her ASIS work would be downgraded. Kim had thought about it and she realised Tammy was right. She wanted out. She wanted out of the army, too. She wanted to settle down, live in one place for more than a month and spend all her free time with Harry.

Harry. It all came back to Harry.

She felt the desolation overwhelm her once more and worked hard to fight it, not wanting to ruin the relaxation she'd been enjoying. Lying on the grass in the middle of the gardens with other people around was not the time to start getting upset and crying her eyes out. Cloud-watching. She would do more cloud-watching until her father arrived and not even *think* about Harry. She sighed again, trying to clear her mind of what had happened.

Kim heard the sound of someone walking close by, but forced herself to remain relaxed. The footsteps stopped and slowly she opened her eyes. A man was standing beside her, bent over, watching her.

She bolted upright in fright, her heart hammering against her ribs, narrowly missing connecting with the man's head.

'Harry!'

'Why is it that every time I get near you, you jump with fright?'

Kim felt her jaw drop and, unable to control herself, she just sat there and stared.

He sat down beside her, *close* beside her, his body facing hers…and he smiled that smile that had the ability to knocked her world off its axis. It wasn't fair.

'How…how did you find me?' she stammered, after drinking her fill of him.

'Your mother.'

'My *mother*!' Her eyebrows hit her hairline.

'Sure. She just called you, didn't she?'

'Yes, but—'

'You think you're the only one who can be a spy?'

'Harry, that's not what—'

He laughed. 'Tammy gave me your parents' address, and when I arrived in Canberra they gave me directions to the gardens, and then your mum phoned just now and told me exactly where to find you.'

'But…you didn't want to…um…want me…' Her words ended in a whisper and tears filled her eyes.

'That's just plain ridiculous.' His voice was soft and he cupped her cheek with his hand. 'Kimberlie, of course I want you. I love you.'

'But…you can't. You hate me and you walked away and—' Her words were cut short as Harry pressed his lips to hers, effectively silencing her. She gasped and leaned into him, unable to believe that this was real, that *he* was real. That he was here. That he wanted her. That he loved her.

It felt so right to be with him once more. Raising her hands, she tentatively touched his hair, the feel of the soft strands beneath her fingertips helping her to realise this wasn't a dream but reality. He was really here.

She sighed and deepened the kiss, drawing him closer, her need for him making her so anxious she thought she was going to burst with happiness. His mouth moved over hers with perfect synchronicity and as she dragged in a breath, the scent of him, which had stayed in her smell receptors and tortured her during the past few weeks, made her feel cherished and alive. *He* made her feel alive.

'Kimberlie,' he groaned, as he eventually wrenched his mouth from hers and buried his head in her neck. 'You smell so good. I've missed that. I've missed you.' He pulled back to look into her desire-filled eyes. 'I've been a fool.'

'No.' She placed a finger over his lips to stop his words. 'No. You were right to walk away. I'd hurt you.'

'Hurt my pride perhaps.' He smiled and the effect burst straight through her, making her feel vibrant and alive.

'Do you know what you do to me when you smile like that?' she gasped, trying to get control of her body.

His smile increased and he raised his eyebrows suggestively, intimating he knew exactly what he was doing to her. 'Do you know what you do to me when you react to my smile?'

'No.' Her eyes widened.

'You make me feel powerful. You make me feel as though I can take on the world, that I can do anything…' He gazed at her mouth, brushing his thumb gently across her lips. When she gasped at his touch, her lips parting ready for his next onslaught, he groaned. 'No woman has ever affected me the way you do,' he whispered, his breath fanning her face. 'You make me feel powerful but at the same time I'm completely at your mercy. I can't get enough. I'm addicted. Wild for you.'

This time, when he pressed his mouth to hers, it was the most possessive kiss she'd ever received. It said he was the only man for her and she was the only woman for him. It was a fact. She welcomed the emotions, not holding anything back, eager to show him how much she really loved him.

The fire that consumed them both was more than just uncontrollable need, more than just a physical attraction, more than just want and desire. It was the be-all and end-all of every emotion either of them had ever experienced. At the absolute worst—between them—it was very good. Now, as they were both on the brink of raging out of control, it was…indescribable.

Finally, he broke the embrace, both of them gasping for oxygen.

'Kimberlie—my love.' His eyes were smouldering with desire and as he swallowed, she watched the action of his Adam's apple and couldn't resist bending to press a kiss to his neck. 'Kimberlie.' He glanced over his shoulder as though he'd just remembered their surroundings. 'I could quite easily get carried away.'

'You and me both!' She leaned forward again and nibbled at his earlobe, delighted when he groaned.

'Kimberlie.' He exhaled harshly and moved away. 'Stop.'

'No. I've been parched, crawling through the desert sand, hoping for an oasis. I've finally found my oasis and I'm not allowed to drink?' She eyed him quizzically. 'You're not just a mirage, are you?'

Harry chuckled. 'No, and I understand your need, but if you drink too much, you'll make yourself sick.'

'Spoilsport.'

'Glutton.'

Kim laughed, feeling the weight of the world lift from her shoulders. Harry was here. Harry wanted her. Harry loved her—of that she was certain, otherwise he wouldn't have come back.

'I can't help it. You're so perfect for me.'

'Yes.' He brushed some curls back from her face, his look intent. 'I love you, Kimberlie Mason, and I need to know if you're going to marry me.'

'Marry you?' Kim couldn't believe what she was hearing. Her laugh was one of amazement as total happiness consumed her. When she looked at him, it was with all the love she possessed shining in her eyes. 'I can think of nothing I want more than to be your wife.'

Air whooshed out of him and she realised he'd been holding his breath. 'Really?'

She laughed again. 'How can you be so unsure? I thought I made you feel powerful, as though you could take on the world.'

'You do, but only if you're right there beside me.' Harry placed a small kiss on her lips and forced himself to stop at that.

Kim smiled. 'Am I that irresistible?'

'Do you really need to ask?'

She sighed and tenderly touched his face. 'I still can't believe you're here.' She thought for a moment. 'Tammy knew? She called me earlier today but I—' She stopped, a little embarrassed to tell him about the emotional mess she'd been because of him.

'You…?' he prompted.

Kim took a deep breath. No more secrets—about anything. 'I couldn't talk to her because I was sobbing my heart out.'

'Ah, Kimberlie.' Harry's gaze was filled with love. 'You make me feel like a real jerk when you say things like that. I knew I should have come sooner but…well, I needed to work things out.'

'I know, and I kept telling myself you had every right to hate me and never want to see me again.'

'I don't hate you,' he reassured her. 'Quite the opposite.' He pressed another quick kiss to her lips. 'I told you about my wife.'

Kim nodded.

'It took quite a number of years after she left for me to even think about dating.' He shook his head. 'Then it seemed that every girl I went out with ended up lying to me.'

'Like Elaine?'

'Exactly.' He paused and held her hands tightly in his. 'When I found out you'd been lying as well, it almost killed me, Kimberlie. You see, you were different—*very* different—from the other women I'd dated. Different because I'd fallen in love with you.

'I'd realised something wasn't right and I kept telling myself to stay away, but I couldn't. By then you'd become addictive and I felt like a complete fool, giving away my heart to a woman who might one day destroy me.'

'Which I did.' Kim's eyes filled with tears.

'No.' He tenderly wiped them away. 'No, honey. You didn't. You may have bruised me a little but you didn't destroy me. That's just one of the things I've realised these past few weeks. Your reasons for deceiving me were honest—which is a bit of an oxymoron, I think, but still... Your motives were honourable. When I realised that, it counted for everything. It showed me your true character.'

'Thank you.' She sniffed and he handed her his handkerchief. 'It's just that I was under orders. I joined the army straight from school, did my medical training with them and have been following orders ever since. I couldn't disobey them.'

'It shows your integrity. You *are* a woman I can trust. You have ethics, morals and values…' He grinned and rubbed the back of his head, a teasing glint in his eyes. 'And a good elbow-to-the-head manoeuvre.'

'Oh, no.' Kim closed her eyes in disgust at her past behaviour. 'I am so sorry.' She opened her eyes. 'I felt so bad. That's why I had to come back and nurse you.'

'Tammy told me.'

'Really? What else did Tammy tell you?'

'You mean when she was guiding me through the mound of paperwork needed to sign me up to ASIS?'

'What?' She stared at him in disbelief. 'When?'

'When what?'

'When did they sign you up?'

'Officially? Last week.'

'Oh, no.' She shook her head. 'No. Trust me, Harry, you do not want to get into this life.'

'Why not? You're in it.'

'Not for much longer. After I had that fight with Kat McPhee, I effectively blew my cover. Now Moss—oh, he's the director of operations—'

'We've met.'

'Oh. Well, Moss said I can only do—'

'Overseas operations from now on. I know. I also know about the camera in the morgue when the autopsy was being performed, which was explained to me when someone from ASIS picked me up and took me to Moss for questioning.'

Kim opened her mouth, then closed it again, frowning. Thoughts were running through her head and she was desperately trying to make sense of them. 'You saw Moss *before* John McPhee's party?'

'Yes.'

'Then you knew about my work?'

'No. I was told they had an operative on the inside. Initially, I thought it was the cleaner at the morgue but it wasn't until the party that I realised the operative was you.'

'Harry, I'm sor—'

He placed two fingers on her lips, silencing her. 'Stop apologising, my love, and let me explain. When I met with Moss, he asked me why I took the sample and I told him.'

'You wanted to check for unauthorised substances.'

'Yes.'

'I knew it. I told them that.'

'So I've realised since. Moss also said the agency had been interested in recruiting me as I work overseas quite a lot. He said I already have the perfect cover but when this business came up about Japarlin, they needed to be one hundred per cent sure I wasn't involved.'

She watched him closely. There was a sparkle in his eyes. 'What else did Moss say?'

'He said if I was recruited, I'd need a partner. Someone who was qualified to practise medicine and who was also an ASIS operative.' Harry's look was intense with meaning.

'Me?'

'You.'

'I'm stunned.' Kim hesitated a moment. 'Is it official?'

'No, but you can be sure I'll be requesting you. I mean, as my wife, it's only natural we'd travel together. You meet both of Moss's requirements so I can't think of any reason why he wouldn't approve it. The only thing I'm still in the dark about are your real qualifications.'

'What? You don't believe I'm a service registrar?'

'Nope. Far too qualified to carry that cover off. That's what tipped me off to you in the first place.' He smiled, and when she didn't return his smile he took her hand in his. 'What's wrong?'

'I don't know if being partners is a good idea. I mean, when Moss told me I was basically useless to him inside Australia, I planned to get out altogether. Quit ASIS and the army. I thought about getting a job in a hospital and just being a normal person.'

To her surprise, Harry laughed. 'Kimberlie, honey, you are *far* from normal. You're unique, special, and I wouldn't want you any other way. You have gifts, you have a natural ability when it comes to intelligence work. Believe me, Moss couldn't speak more highly of you.'

'Really?' Kim was taken aback.

'You can't honestly tell me you don't enjoy the work you've done with ASIS?'

'Well…I do but…I've come to realise there are more important things in life.'

'Like what? Settling down to a normal routine? Honey, you'd be bored inside a month.'

'Do you really think so?'

'I know so, because I'm the same. Why do you think I do those clinics overseas? I need a release from the daily grind. I want to help people who can't afford proper treatment but those clinics also help me. The keep me focused on what's important in life. Being involved with ASIS is another way I can help, and with you by my side the current void in my life will be filled—the part where I've found my one true love.' He brushed a brief kiss across her lips and the touch reassured her. 'Now, tell me what's really wrong.'

She was amazed at how well he knew her. 'I love you, Harry, which is why I'm not sure I can work with you as my ASIS partner. I mean, what if you get hurt? I'd fall to pieces.'

'Just like you did with Chris?'

'Yes,' she said urgently. 'It was horrible and it took me years to get over his senseless death.'

'He died trying to save other people. Some would call that bravery.'

'Some. Others would call it foolhardy. You must *always* note the danger to yourself and those around you. Chris not only endangered himself but me as well. He compromised the mission and blew our cover. I was so cross with him for so long, which only made me feel more guilty. I can't go through anything like that again, Harry. I just can't. I love you far too much.' She grabbed him close, happy when he reciprocated by holding her firmly.

'It won't happen, Kimberlie.'

'How can you be so sure? You went across the road into that burning building, didn't you?'

'That was different, honey,' he said softly. 'I'd weighed up the risks, the pros and cons. I could have broken my way into the apartment, but I didn't. I knew the wisest course of action was to wait for reinforcements and so I did. I'm not looking to be a hero, Kimberlie and neither are you. Because of that, we have a good opportunity to make a difference in the world. Isn't that why you got into this game in the first place? To make a difference? Besides, there's risk in everything, but if we both keep our heads and listen to each other, I know we'll be fine.'

'What about children?'

Harry pulled back to look at her. 'You want a family?'

'Yes. Don't you?'

'Of course, but I just…well, for some reason I thought you were the career-woman type who didn't want children.' He shook his head. 'There's still so much we need to learn about each other.'

'So? What about children?'

'When the children come along, things will be different. That's when I suggest we both quit being field operatives and if we still want to work with ASIS, we do so from an analytical point of view.' He placed his hands on her shoulders and the look he gave her was one of complete confidence. 'We can do this, Kimberlie.'

'And if I quit the army?'

'Not a problem, so long as you're doing it for the right reasons.'

'I don't want to travel any more,' she said simply. 'I want to be with you, in Sydney. I want to go overseas and help you with your clinics, to make a difference in the world.'

'Then that's what we do. I can get you a job at Sydney General…uh, if I knew your real qualifications.'

She smiled, feeling as though yet another weight had been lifted off her shoulders. 'You are so good for me.' She kissed him and when she tried to linger, he groaned and eased away.

'Stop trying to change the subject. Answer the question.'

'I hold a degree in general surgery as well as a diploma in orthopaedics and a diploma in general medicine.'

'You're *that* qualified?' Harry was surprised.

'You know how it is when you're overseas, you become a "bitsa" doctor, covering a bit of everything. I've even had to do tooth extractions and ingrown toenails.'

'Sounds like fun, Dr Mason, or should that be *Mr* Mason, as you're a qualified surgeon? Better yet, surprise me and tell me you've done your Ph.D.'

She laughed and shook her head. 'No…but I've been considering it.'

'Perhaps you can do it when the kids are young?'

'I like the way you think, Dr Buchanan. So, when do you want these children?'

'Not for a few more years, if that's all right with you.' Harry gathered her close. 'I want you all to myself for a while.'

Kim's answer was to press her lips lovingly to his. The instant they made contact, her phone buzzed to life. 'It's my mum,' she said, reading the display before answering the call.

'Kimmy?' Her mother was a little hesitant. 'Still all right?'

Kim laughed. 'Everything's perfect, Mum.'

Eileen sighed. 'Harry found you, then?'

'He most certainly did. I take it this means Dad isn't coming to pick me up?'

'Er…no, dear. So everything's perfect, is it? He seems like a very nice young man. Handsome and tall, too. I like tall men. Do I start planning the wedding?'

'Yes, Mum. Start planning the wedding,' she said with a grin at Harry. A moment later she disconnected the call, deafened by her mother's excited squeal. 'There's no backing out now.'

Harry nodded, his face solemn. 'Your parents don't know about ASIS, do they.' It was a statement, not a question.

'No.' He nodded again but she felt his disapproval. 'I'm protecting them, Harry. Think of how your mother or your sister would react if you told them you'd just been recruited by the country's secret service. ASIS has a lot of enemies and sometimes they're willing to make statements by taking it out on people closest to their operatives. If the time came to tell them, I would, without hesitation, but until then I want them protected. Besides, I consider it a gesture of love to deceive those I care about the most.'

'Like you did with me.'

'Yes, like I did with you, even though I was desperate to tell you.'

'And Tammy was listening to our…er… conversations all the time?'

Kim smiled. 'Most of the time. We've known each other for so long and she knew when to go radio silent, but I'll tell you, I was so glad Tammy was my partner for that operation because she was the one who told me to go for it every time I tried to deny my growing feelings for you.

'Remind me to thank her one day.'

'Let's make her bridesmaid and make her wear a really frilly dress.'

Harry laughed. 'I don't think that would suit her.'

Kim's grin was pure teasing. 'I know.'

'Now, another thing. You are going to teach me those martial arts moves you know, aren't you? I still owe you a whack to the back of the head.'

Kim shook her head in embarrassment. 'Are you ever going to let me forget that?'

'No. I like it when you're flustered.'

'Well, I can think of quite a few better…' she trailed her fingernail down his cheek '…more satisfying ways for you to get me flustered.' Her finger traced the outline of his lips and he caught her finger in his mouth and sucked it gently. Kim's heart skipped a beat and she gasped. 'See?' The word came out as a breathless moan.

'I think the time has come for us to leave such a public place because I don't think I can hold onto my restraint much longer.' Harry gave her a hard, possessive kiss before helping her to her feet. 'And I haven't even asked about your ankle, although I heard it wasn't broken.'

She smiled as she leaned against him. 'Badly bruised and still a lovely shade of purple, blue and green.'

'Splendid.' They headed to his car and once they were seated he started the engine and pulled out of the car park.

'Where are we going?' she asked when he missed the turn-off to her parents' house.

'To buy you an engagement ring. Although, please, don't chose something that sticks up too far. I wouldn't want you to scratch me when we're practising our martial arts sparring.'

Kim laughed. 'Harry!' She smiled and placed her hand possessively on his leg.

Harry. Her whole happiness came back to Harry...and he was all *hers*.